"I understand from this you," nodding toward Waggit, "that your living situation has become difficult."

"It's the Uprights," growled Tazar. "It's always the Uprights. They cannot tolerate anything they cannot control, and free dogs are intolerable to them."

"It has always been so," said Beidel. "We live among them more than you do, but we have adapted to their ways."

"We have as well, wherever possible," agreed Tazar, "but when their ways take the very food upon which you survive, or when their ways trap you and take you to the Great Unknown, then you cannot adapt. Aside from your generosity in lending us this feeder, we have very little food. Unless we can resolve our problems soon, we will starve."

"Are you willing to consider any other options?" asked Beidel.

"Consider, yes," Tazar answered. "I am a dog of action, but I am also careful in my actions. I will not expose my team to reckless danger."

"Very noble," said Beidel. "But in these matters there is a level of risk you have to accept. My team has saved many dogs from circumstances far worse than yours, and we can do the same for you if you trust us."

ALSO BY PETER HOWE

Waggit's Tale

Waggit Again

WAGGIT FOREVER

PETER HOWE

WAGGIT
FOREVER

Drawings by
Omar Rayyan

HARPER
An Imprint of HarperCollinsPublishers

Waggit Forever

Text copyright © 2010 by Peter Howe

Illustrations copyright © 2010 by Omar Rayyan

www.harpercollinschildrens.com

Library of Congress Cataloging-in-Publication Data

Howe, Peter.

Waggit forever / by Peter Howe ; [illustrations by Omar Rayyan].
— 1st ed.

p. cm.

Summary: When a shortage of food and too many humans make it
impossible for Waggit and his friends to survive in the city park, they
make a dangerous journey, guided by a team of street dogs, in search of
a new place to live.

ISBN 978-0-06-176516-2

[1. Dogs—Fiction.] I. Rayyan, Omar, ill. II. Title.

PZ7.H8377Wae 2010   2009023547

[Fic]—dc22   CIP

                                                    AC

Typography by Amy Ryan

11 12 13 14 15 CG/CW 10 9 8 7 6 5 4 3 2 1

❖

First paperback edition, 2011

This book is dedicated to the Good Uprights who devote their lives to the welfare of all creatures, and especially to those who rescue dogs from the Great Unknown.

TABLE OF CONTENTS

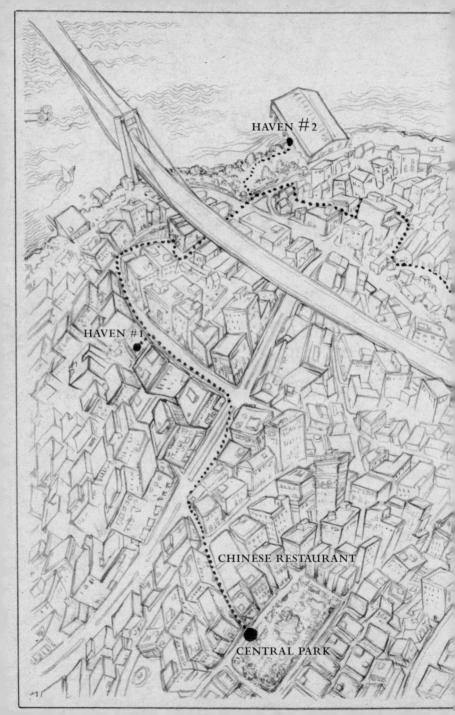

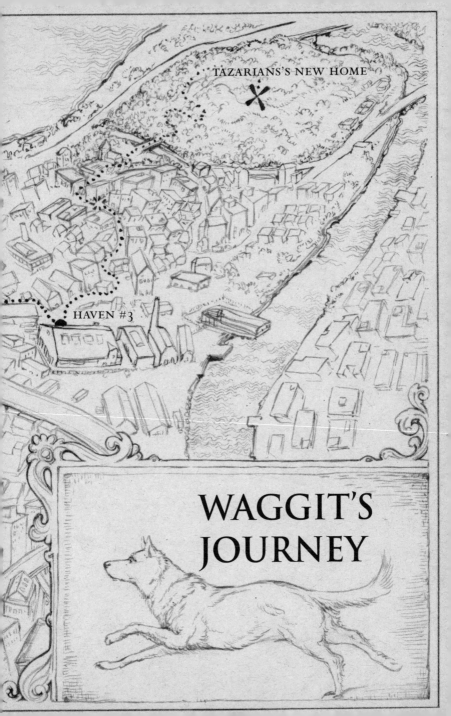

TAZARIANS'S NEW HOME

HAVEN #3

WAGGIT'S
JOURNEY

1
Hunger Pangs

Lowdown sighed and laid his head on his paws.

"It's all over," he growled, in an uncharacteristically gloomy voice.

"What is?" asked Waggit, disturbed by his friend's mood.

"Life as we know it," said Lowdown. "Just look at them. Wherever you look they're doing stuff: fixing things, clearing bushes, changing everything. Nothing good'll come of it, you mark my words."

The two dogs viewed the activities of the park

workers from a vantage point in one of the scrubby bushes that still remained. They were members of a pack of dogs that lived in the park by themselves, without the company of humans, using their own wits to survive. The authorities described them as "wild" and "a menace," although it would be hard to imagine two less ferocious or threatening dogs than Waggit and Lowdown. Waggit was a young, creamy white animal of uncertain breeding, like most of the dogs in the pack, and certainly like his best friend, Lowdown, who had very short legs—for which he was named—and always looked as if he'd just gotten up. He was very old and had lived all his life in the park. Although Lowdown was cynical by nature, he was rarely as depressed as he seemed to be today. Waggit could see that the park was changing, but it hardly seemed to forecast the doom that Lowdown described.

"They're just cleaning things up a bit," the younger dog said cheerfully. "It's not like they're making the park smaller."

"Maybe," said Lowdown, "but as soon as they've opened up the paths and fixed all the broken stuff, the Uprights'll come flooding in here, you mark my words. You show Uprights an empty space, and they'll come and sit in it or throw balls at each other. Then the next thing you know, the Ruzelas will be all fired up, trying to catch *us* in order to protect *them*, and we was here first."

It was true that one of the things that made this part of the park an ideal place to live was that very few human beings ventured into its wild reaches. And if there were no people, there were fewer park rangers to harass the pack of stray dogs to which Waggit and Lowdown belonged, a team called the Tazarians, named after their fearless leader, Tazar. When Waggit thought back, he realized it had been a similar effort to clean up the park that had caused them to move from their previous location farther south. Their old home, an abandoned tunnel, had been turned into a storage shed housing lawn mowers, leaf blowers, and other tools that kept that part of the park in its newly pristine condition.

The move north had proved to be successful. Known to the team as the Deepwoods End, it was wilder and, as its name implied, much more heavily wooded, with thicker underbrush. This not only kept the humans away, but it also provided a home for the small animals that were the dogs' main source of food. The area even had streams and ponds from which the team members could drink and in which they could play. All in all, it was as close to an ideal life as homeless dogs in the middle of a big city could hope for.

"But even if they clean it up," mused Waggit, after thinking about it for a while, "they probably won't cut down all the trees. I mean, they wouldn't, would they?"

"There's no telling what Uprights will do," said Lowdown glumly. "At the very least life will change. It's bound to."

It was in this despondent frame of mind that the two animals returned to their home, a large drainage pipe that at one time had emptied water into one of the many pools in the area. At some point in its past it had broken and no longer functioned, but it made a very decent home for all the dogs, except for Lowdown, who was too old. His actual age remained a mystery, but most of his teeth were worn down, patches of fur were missing, and he had arthritis that caused him pain. His frail condition made it impossible for him to climb in and out of the pipe, so he had found a home in the bowl of a dead tree not far away.

When the two friends arrived back at the clearing

near the entrance to the pipe, the other team members did nothing to lighten their mood. It was one of those days when everything seemed to be going wrong.

If you were a free dog and lived without humans, your number one priority was always food. Meals came in two ways: hunting or foraging. Before they were forced north into the Deepwoods End, the dogs could rely on human wastefulness as a source of food. There were always leftovers from the restaurant in the park; the food vendors with their carts regularly threw away goods at the end of the day; park visitors filled trash cans with discarded food. But where the dogs lived now was far from these sources, so they mostly relied on hunting. This was not a problem, because the conditions that made the Deepwoods a good place for dogs to live benefited small animals as well, and so the hunting was relatively easy—but not recently, and certainly not today.

"I can't believe it," complained Cal. "It wasn't that I was hunting bad—it's that I wasn't hunting at all. There was nothing."

"I think I saw one scurry the whole time we was out," said Raz, Cal's closest friend and constant companion. "He didn't look too fat either."

"Where have they all gone?" asked Lady Magica, one of the team's three females and an accomplished hunter. "The Deepwoods used to be thick with them." It was true that when the team first moved to their present location, they would choose what they wanted to eat that night and then go looking for it. It was almost like having a menu. Nowadays they had to take what they could get.

"It's all this cleaning up that's caused it," grumbled Lowdown, "all this chopping and fixing and sweeping."

"I blame the youngsters," said Gruff, the team curmudgeon, who was bad tempered at the best of times. "They ain't got the fortitude we had when I was a pup." Nobody was quite sure what this had to do with anything, but since Gruff always blamed the woes of the world on the younger generation, they paid him no attention.

Just then a cheery voice was heard above their heads.

"Oh my, oh my, what a sad and sorry team I have."

They looked up to see their leader, Tazar, standing proudly upon the rock that formed one side of the clearing. He was a magnificent, strong black dog with an impressive plumed tail. There were now many more gray hairs around his mouth and nose than when Waggit had first met him, but these only seemed to increase his dignity and authority. He leaped from the rock with an agility that showed no sign of age.

"Why all the drooping whiskers?" he asked with a chuckle. "What disaster has befallen you all? Has Gordo lost weight, or is it something more tragic?"

"No, boss, he ain't," said Lowdown. "But he might if we don't get any food soon—like we all might, and I ain't got it to lose."

Gordo was an enormously overweight dog who never seemed to get any slimmer however meager the team's rations got. If he ever became skinny, it would be a sure sign that the team was in desperate trouble.

"No luck hunting today?" Tazar inquired.

"Nothing," replied Cal. "We never saw nothing."

"It's probably just a temporary anomaly," said Tazar, who loved long words and even knew what some of them meant. "More than likely it's just seasonal."

"I don't know what season that would be, boss," Lowdown remarked. "We're in the Warming. It's not even the Long Light yet, and no animal slumbers before the Chill, no matter how small they are."

It was true that those creatures that hibernated

would wait until after the first frost before burrowing down for the winter. Tazar was determinedly upbeat, however, and he wasn't going to let Lowdown's logic destroy his good mood. He also knew that keeping up the dogs' morale was his responsibility as their leader.

"Well," he cried, "even if there's no prey, we're coming into the Long Light, and that means plenty of Uprights, and Uprights mean waste, which means full trash cans and Dumpsters, so, dogs, let's scavenge."

But Tazar's enthusiasm fell on deaf ears. Despair is often infectious, like measles, and most of the team seemed truly affected—even Waggit, although he tried to hide it.

"I'm up for it," he said to Tazar. "Where shall we start?"

"Hmm," Tazar murmured. "Well, where do *you* think would be good, Waggit?"

This was a technique of Tazar's that the team knew well. If he had no idea of the answer to a question, he would turn it around by asking one of his own. In this manner not only did he never have to admit he didn't know something, but it gave the appearance of caring about what the other team members thought.

"Well," Waggit answered, "that's the problem,

Tazar. We've already checked out the trash cans around here, and there's nothing worth considering in them."

"Nothing?" Tazar said with surprise. "No half-eaten sausages? No crusts of bread? No cheese? No discarded hamburgers?"

As he went through this litany of food choices, he could see the distress on the faces of the dogs in front of him. Some were drooling, and Gordo looked as if he were in actual pain just thinking about such morsels.

"Don't go on, Tazar," the chubby animal pleaded with his leader. "There's nothing in them at all. Trust me on this."

Since Gordo was the team authority on the subject, Tazar reluctantly believed him. He turned to Cal, Raz, and Lady Magica.

"And you say you saw nothing worth hunting?" he asked them.

"Nothing," replied Cal, "not even a nibbler."

"Not even a flea," said Raz.

"Oh," wheezed Lowdown with a chuckle, ferociously scratching beneath his chin, "I could've given you a lifetime supply of those if you'd only asked."

Tazar, however, was not amused. He knew only too

well how team morale could be affected by hunger, how restless and bad tempered they would get if they went too long without food. It was during one such bleak period that Gordo had nearly killed both Lady Magica and himself by sharing a rat with her that he claimed to have hunted, when in fact park workers had poisoned it. Something had to be done, thought Tazar, and quickly.

The decision as to what exactly that would be was put on hold by the breathless arrival of Lady Alona.

The dogs who made their home in the park were divided into two distinct groups: team dogs and loners. Loners, as their name implies, lived by themselves, hunted by themselves, and had little contact with any other dogs. Their solitary existence was hard. It was difficult to hunt alone, and they were more easily captured in the sweeps that the park rangers did from time to time to round up stray dogs and take them to the pound. It was during one such action that a shy female had come to the team and asked to join them. She had been a loner for as long as she could remember, but now she wanted the security that being a team member would give her.

The Tazarians gladly took her in and gave her the

unimaginative name Alona. Because of their isolated lifestyle, loners were always socially awkward, often eccentric, and frequently suspicious. This was true of Alona. She took some time to fit in, but now she played an important role that was somewhere between a team dog and a solitary one. While she lived as a Tazarian, she also spent many hours by herself, scouring the park for information and gossip, and she was a valuable source of intelligence, often giving them crucial warning of events that would affect their lives. Now as she caught her breath, the dogs gathered around, eager to hear what she had to say.

"It's Olang, sir," she finally said to Tazar. "Your son."

The atmosphere suddenly went electric with tension. Alona had just uttered the word that no dog ever said in Tazar's company. It was the name of his estranged son, who had left the group to lead a rival team that was the Tazarians' bitter enemy.

"I have no son," Tazar growled, his eyes blazing with anger. "That treacherous, deceitful wretch is nothing to me now."

"Yes, sir, I understand," said Alona, "but he and his team are suffering as we are, and he wishes to have a war council with you, leader to leader. He says that this situation will never be resolved unless the teams work together."

"The words that come out of his miserable, lying mouth are of no consequence to me," Tazar snarled.

"That may be so, sir, but the actions he takes could affect all of us." One of the advantages of Alona's complete lack of social awareness was that she would often continue a conversation with Tazar well past the point beyond which other dogs would dare to go.

"How so?" inquired Tazar.

"Well, sir, you know Olang," she replied. "He could cause a whole heap of trouble that we'd be blamed for as much as his team."

"I also know," said Tazar, "that talking to him is a waste of time and breath."

Now it was Waggit's turn to join in.

"Tazar, you're right," he said. "But even if you can't change his behavior, it would be good to know what he intends to do."

"Waggit's got a point, boss," Lowdown chimed in. "What've you got to lose?"

"What I've got to lose," snapped Tazar, "is my peace of mind and my equanimity."

"If you don't mind me saying so, boss," Lowdown continued, "I don't know what equa-thingummy is, but your mind ain't too peaceful right now, so you might as well meet with him and get it over with."

And so it was that Alona was sent back into the woods to seek out one of Olang's lieutenants and arrange a meeting between the two leaders—a meeting that everyone knew would be fraught with hostility and mistrust.

2

Tazar Makes a Plan

Because of the urgency of the situation facing the two teams, the encounter was arranged for the day following Tazar's reluctant agreement to meet. The site chosen for the occasion was a large outcrop of rock overlooking the road that ran within the park. The arrangement was that the teams would stay on opposite sides in the heavily wooded areas that bordered it, while the leaders and their principal deputies would be the only dogs to come face-to-face on the outcrop.

Tazar, accompanied by Waggit and Lowdown,

arrived early. The big black dog felt that there was an advantage to be had by staking claim to a position, thereby forcing his opponents to take the only spot left. He made sure that the sun, which was shining brightly that day, would be in his adversaries' eyes. But even with his advanced planning, Tazar was restless and irritable. It would be the first time that he had met with his son since Olang's defection, and the anger Tazar felt toward him had not diminished over time. Suddenly he stood up, his tail and ears erect and the hair on his back bristling with tension.

Scrambling up the side of the rock came Olang. He was an impressively ferocious dog, heavily muscled and, like his father, completely black, except that he had a large white patch over one eye that was strangely disconcerting. Accompanying him were his two sidekicks, Wilbur, who had been the evil lieutenant of the team's former leader, Tashi, and a new dog none of the Tazarians knew. He was called Whippety Will and was the thinnest dog Waggit had ever seen. He looked like a fur-covered skeleton, as if he had no flesh on his bones at all. Even his tail was like a rat's, and he shivered constantly, although it was a warm spring day. Whether his emaciated body was the result of starvation or simply his natural state was hard to tell, but neither Olang nor Wilbur looked like they needed feeding up.

"Father," Olang said when all three were on top of the rock, "how are you? You look good; older but good."

Despite his size and ferocious look Olang had a thin, reedy voice that sounded whiny and sarcastic at the same time.

"I didn't come here to exchange pleasantries with you, Olang," Tazar snarled. "I came to see what solutions, if any, you and your miserable companions have to this situation that we all face."

"My, my, Father." Olang smirked, appearing to enjoy the effect his presence had on Tazar. "This hostility will get us nowhere. I came here in the spirit of friendly cooperation and hoped that you would too."

Waggit stepped in between them.

"We want to see if there is a way we can all continue to live in the park in peace, and if that means we must pool our resources, then so be it," he said.

"Ah," sneered Olang, "the saintly Waggit, the dog of dogs, the peacemaker. I doubt that any wussy ideas you have would appeal to us in any way. We are dogs of action, not pretty speeches."

"It's your actions that worry me," said Tazar. "All you know is how to fight."

"Sometimes, dear Father," Olang said, "that is all you need to know."

"Gentledogs, gentledogs." Now it was Wilbur's turn to speak, and he did so in his usual sly manner. "Let's discuss this matter openly and frankly. We will tell you how we see things, and we will be more than willing to listen to any ideas that your team may have." Those who had ever had any dealings with Wilbur knew that the last qualities you would associate with him were openness and frankness. "As we see it," he continued, "the main problem we have is the one we always have—the Uprights. Get rid of the Uprights, and you solve all your troubles. Why is there no prey? The Uprights. Who persecutes us and takes us to the Great Unknown? The Uprights. Who tries to kill us with their rollers? The Uprights. Who controls most of the park now? The Uprights. It is time for us to take a stand. If we let them take over the Deepwoods End, we will have run out of places to move to. This is our last chance to protect what is rightfully ours."

"What you don't realize," said Tazar, "and what you

have never accepted, is that the Uprights *do* control everything. There is nothing they cannot do if they have a mind to. What we must do is to find ways to live given that simple fact. Declaring war on them is not an option."

"Not declaring war, Father," Olang said with fake astonishment, as if this were the last thing he was thinking. "Not war, but hit-and-run tactics. An attack here, an attack there, and pretty soon all those Uprights who are sweeping and sawing and chopping down will be too scared to come to work. Then they'll leave us alone, and the bushes will grow back and the animals will return and only then will we be able to live in the peace and harmony that Waggit's wimpy heart longs for."

"And if your team joined forces with ours," Wilbur said in his smarmiest voice, "then we would have the power to spread terror throughout the Deepwoods."

Slowly and deliberately, Tazar got up. He shook himself and then turned to Lowdown and Waggit.

"Come on," he commanded. "Let's go. There's no point in talking with dogs who think only with their teeth."

"Is our plan too much for you, Father?" Olang asked

with a contemptuous growl. "Does it take too much courage?"

"Your plan is worthless; not because it requires too much courage," Tazar replied, "but because it requires too little common sense."

As the three of them moved out, Olang, Wilbur, and Whippety Will backed off as if expecting an attack at any moment. Instead, Tazar paused in front of Olang and spoke to him in a quiet but firm voice.

"You took over leadership of this team when Tashi was killed in a fight with me, even though I was not the one to put an end to him. I hoped that you had learned a lesson from that experience, that you would have realized violence only brings more violence. But no; it seems that you are Tashi's son more than mine, and you will likely meet the same end."

The power and emotion of Tazar's words left the other dogs speechless. As the Tazarians walked away, they heard Olang mutter a single word: "Pathetic!"

Nobody talked while they made their way home. The dogs could sense the anger that Tazar was feeling. It was the first time that he had sat face-to-face with his son since that terrible day when he and Tashi, the former leader of the rival team, had fought. It was a tragedy that had cost the lives of two dogs, Tashi himself and another called Lug, one of the Tazarians. It was also the day when Olang had abandoned his father forever. The team suspected that ever since then, Tazar had kept hoping his wayward son would eventually come to his senses and return to the group, maybe bringing the other team with him and thereby ending the hostilities that had plagued park life for as long as any dog could remember. But nothing had changed.

Tazar was still in a dark mood when they arrived back at the pipe, and most of the dogs avoided him. They knew it was better to leave him alone when he was like this. Finally, Lowdown broke the silence. He was the only one in the team who seemed to be completely unfazed by Tazar's fury.

"The thing is," he said, "Olang's plan was stupid, but it was a plan."

"I wouldn't call it a plan," retorted Tazar brusquely. "Plans require thought. That was just blind retaliation."

"But my point is," Lowdown persisted, "we don't have anything better."

Tazar pierced him with a glowering stare that would

have made any other dog cringe and slink away.

"Just because *you* don't know what I intend to do," he said, "doesn't mean that *I* don't know what I intend to do."

"I knew you'd have a plan," said Waggit, trying to defuse a tense situation. "Tell us what it is."

Tazar thought for a while, and then said: "The food won't come to us, so we must go to the food. There's still food in the park, just not in this part of it. We must go to where it is—to the Skyline End."

"But boss," protested Lowdown, "the Skyline's thick with Uprights."

"That's why it's also thick with food," said Tazar.

"Does that mean we have to move?" Gordo asked glumly. "I've started to like living in the pipe."

"It's a wonder you can get in and out, there's so much of you," screeched Lady Alicia, who was proud of being the slenderest dog in the team with the possible exception of Waggit.

"Gordo's right," said Gruff. "It's okay to expect young pups to keep moving all over the park, but for us older dogs—to be honest with you, I don't think I have the energy."

"No," Tazar assured them, "we don't have to move;

we just have to organize our food supply a little differently, that's all."

The leader went on to explain his plan. He acknowledged that scavenging in the Skyline End would be more dangerous and that there was no point in risking the safety of the whole team. Only the youngest and fastest dogs would be required to actually gather the food, which they would then bring back to a designated place halfway between the two ends of the park. From here other members of the team would ferry it back to the pipe. It would take longer and be more dangerous, but what alternative did they have?

"Where will the drop-off for the food be?" Waggit asked, ever the practical one.

"We'll use the Goldenside," Tazar answered him. "You remember the place where Tashi and his team lived before they were captured by the Ruzelas?"

The dogs nodded. It was a large clump of bushes that formed a sort of leafy cave. Because it lacked a good escape route, the park rangers had found it easy to round up Tashi's team during one of their periodic sweeps for strays. The only two dogs who had avoided being captured were Tashi himself and Wilbur, his evil lieutenant, who both happened to be in the woods at the time.

"It was a stupid place to try to live," Tazar continued, "but it's more than enough protection to hide the food for a while."

"Can me and Raz be part of the scavengers?" asked Cal, who always found the Skyline End exciting and regretted the fact that they seldom went there now that they lived in the Deepwoods.

"I expect you both to be the leaders of the scavengers," Tazar assured them.

Being the leaders of anything was a novel concept for the two friends, and they yipped with pride and excitement.

"Do we get to give Waggit orders?" Raz asked.

"No you do not," said Lady Magica, "and be careful. Remember what happened when Cal nearly got caught at the Skyline and cut his paw?"

"Ah, if they're stupid enough to want to do it, let them, I say," shrieked Alicia. "Somebody has to and it ain't gonna be me."

"Mommy Magica," pleaded Little One, "can we be . . ."

". . . part of the scavengers?" Little Two finished off Little One's sentence, as he often did.

"Absolutely not," Magica insisted. "You're far too young."

"Magica," said Tazar, "look at them. They're bigger than you and far stronger. They should be contributing to the team. Let them be part of it—they'll be fine."

"Very well then," Magica grudgingly agreed, "but on one condition: that I'm on the scavenging team as well."

Magica knew full well that Tazar didn't have to ask her permission to assign Little One and Little Two to any duty that he wanted. Although she had cared for them like a mother since they were tiny, they weren't her puppies.

"No," said Tazar quietly but firmly. "You'll be of more help organizing the transportation of the food."

"I don't know," muttered Gruff, "but it seems to me you'll want one animal with a brain among the scavengers, 'cause there ain't one now. Magica may be a bit mushy at times, but at least her head's screwed on straight, which is more than you can say about the rest of them."

But Tazar was firm in his decision. Cal, Raz, Little One, and Little Two would be the scavenging party and would be supervised by Waggit; Lady Magica, Gordo, and Alona would be responsible for the transportation of the food from the Goldenside to the Deepwoods; Lowdown and Gruff would guard the pipe, and Alicia would do what Alicia always did—nothing. Tazar himself would coordinate the whole operation, moving back and forth between the Skyline End, the Goldenside, and the Deepwoods as necessary.

"So," Tazar said with satisfaction, "we have a plan and we have our assignments. Now all we need is a little luck."

But the team would soon discover that luck, like food, was in short supply that season.

3

Tazar's Desperate Decision

The first thing that went wrong was a matter of timing. The evening that the team decided to try out the new system was the worst they could have chosen. It was one of the nights that free concerts were held in the park. These were very popular, and the entire Skyline End was full of thousands of people. In some ways this could be a good thing, because there would be much more food dropped on the ground or in trash cans, but the problem was getting to it. The hit-and-run techniques that the dogs had perfected wouldn't work in crowds of this density. You couldn't even hit and walk surrounded by so many people, and on top of that there were many more park rangers and policemen assigned to crowd control and security. The best they could find that night was some sad remains of takeout meals that had been thrown into one of the trash cans at the edge of the park by fans on their way to the concert.

However, it seemed that there would be plenty for all the following day. The crowds were gone, but the amount of trash they left was so monumental that the sanitation workers couldn't possibly collect it all that night. Tazar realized this and got the team out early in the morning. Although this was a much safer time to scavenge, it would normally have produced very little in the way of results because the cans were emptied at night and usually didn't start filling up until the afternoon. Today, however, the mountains of garbage meant that the pickings would be easy.

But still, the scavengers had to be cautious at all times. The early risers going to their jobs were not a problem; they were in too much of a hurry to be bothered by a dog with its head in a trash can. It was the park workers who were the real threat, most of them on machines that were either blowing or mowing. They got bored easily, and the excitement of a dog chase was a welcome distraction. The dogs had to use whatever cover they could in order to get to the trash cans and then quickly retreat with their loot. Despite these hazards, the pile of goodies hidden in the bushes on the Goldenside continued to grow throughout the day. Tazar bustled back and forth along the entire length of the park, instructing Magica and Alona on the best way to get it back to the pipe, while Gordo guarded what they couldn't carry. Because dogs can't hold much in their mouths, it was going to be a long job, and Tazar was eager to finish before nightfall.

On one of the many journeys they made back to the pipe, Magica carried an almost full bag of potato chips in her mouth, and Alona two half-eaten hot dogs. The smell and taste of the food were overpowering, but the number one rule of the team was that all food was shared, and breaking this rule could lead to exile. When they got to the pipe, they left the goods under the watchful eye of Lowdown.

When they returned to the bushes on the

Goldenside, Gordo was nowhere to be seen, but just as they were going to go back into the leafy hiding place for their second load, he came lumbering up.

"I showed him," he said to them.

"You showed who what?" asked Magica.

"That Whippety Will in Tashi's team—I mean Olang's team," he replied. "I showed him you can't insult a Tazarian and get away with it."

The two females glanced at each other in alarm.

"What happened, Gordo?" Magica asked in as calm a voice as she could manage.

"That miserable bundle of skin and bones told me that I was fat but soon I'd be thin because Tazarians are so stupid that Olang's team will get all the food in the park, and they ain't gonna leave any for us, and that we'll all be begging the Ruzelas to take us to the Great Unknown soon just so's we can get a meal. But I showed him," Gordo said proudly.

"Oh dear. How exactly did you show him?" inquired Alona.

"I chased him," Gordo replied, "and I chased him good. Funny thing is, I assumed he would be much faster than me, what with him carrying no weight and all, but he ain't. I almost caught him two or three times, and we was way over by the Risingside before he got away."

Just then the three dogs heard a rustling sound behind them. They whirled around to see a dog running from the bushes with a bag of French fries in his mouth. He was clearly one of Olang's team, recognizable by the missing piece of his ear. Their former leader, Tashi, had insisted that team members let him bite off the end of one ear as a sign of loyalty. It was a practice that Olang had continued when he had taken over control after Tashi's violent death. As the dog disappeared into the woods, Magica, Alona, and Gordo ran over to the bushes and saw what they had feared. The pile of food so painstakingly collected during the day was gone, stolen by the Olangsters. All that was left was half a moldy loaf of bread. It was clear to all of them that Whippety Will's insults had been a diversion to make sure that the food was left unguarded, and while Gordo had lumbered after him, his teammates had transported the food to their own lair.

Just as they were making this discovery, the scavengers returned.

"Well, that's it for the day," said Cal. "They've got

those big rollers that take more trash than you've ever seen. They eat more than Gordo!"

He grinned but then noticed the glum faces of the others.

"Whassup?" he asked.

They told him what had happened—that all the risks they had taken were for almost nothing, in fact worse than nothing, because their enemies were now enjoying the food they had collected. Gordo felt terrible about his stupidity, but it was hard for any of the dogs to be mad at him for long. He wasn't the smartest creature around, but he was generous and good-natured, and everyone on the team liked him, with the possible exceptions of Alicia and Gruff, but then they were always the exceptions when it came to showing their feelings for others.

It was a sorry group that made its way back to the pipe. The thought of yet another day with little food, as well as the fact that the Olangsters were sleeping with full stomachs, depressed everyone. They all knew that the concert had offered a one-time opportunity for a feast and that it had slipped through their paws. Sadly, their luck didn't change in the next few days. It seemed that the team couldn't catch a break, whatever they did. Little One and Little Two were nearly hit by a car when they ran across the road as a worker from the café near the boating pond chased them. They weren't injured, but Little Two dropped the food he had just "found," and it was flattened under the wheels of the car.

Waggit also had a close encounter while trying to pull some pizza out of a trash can. The technique he used on these tall containers was to stand up on his hind legs, hook his front paws over its edge, and then pull it down toward him. This time, unfortunately, the trash can was fastened to a bench. The chain was short and Waggit had trouble getting the container close enough to the ground for easy access. Instead he had to crawl in and reach down to the bottom, and he suddenly found himself stuck in the trash can. Rescue came when an old lady poked him in his rear end with her umbrella while shouting at him to get away, which was precisely what he was trying to do anyway. She jabbed him so hard that the trash can tipped sideways, dumping him on the ground, but without the pizza.

That evening the dogs gathered around the entrance to the pipe as they usually did. What was different about tonight was the silence. None of them spoke, and most chewed on sticks or grass, anything that would take their minds off their hunger. With a worried frown on his face, Tazar took one look at them and decided what they had to do. Desperate times demanded desperate measures.

"We must go outside the park boundaries."

Everyone gasped.

"Boss," said Lowdown, "we don't never go beyond the walls. It's too dangerous, and besides, it ain't our territory."

"We moved our realm up to the Deepwoods End because the Uprights were making it too hard to live in the tunnel," replied Tazar, "and now they're making it too hard to live up here. It may not be our domain, but what choice do we have?'

There was silence as the dogs thought about this. None of them could come up with an alternative to Tazar's suggestion, even though it would have been unthinkable only a few months ago. The park had always provided for their needs—not always in the way they would have wanted, but they had survived. There were months during the winter when there was nothing to hunt and little to scavenge, but Tazar was a prudent leader and would make sure that some food was put away in a stash, usually a hole in the ground where the freezing temperatures would prevent it from spoiling. Besides, the dogs expected to be hungry in the winter; but this was spring, almost summer, a time when the small animals were usually out of hibernation and scuttling around just waiting to be hunted.

Waggit broke the silence.

"There might not be any choice," he said, "but it's still dangerous."

"So's starving," Tazar assured him, and that ended the discussion.

And so it was that Waggit found himself that evening at the back entrance of a Chinese restaurant about a block west of the park. His mission was to scout out the area and find the spots worthy of scavenging. He had been chosen for this duty because his experience in the world outside was greater than any of the other Tazarians. Most of them had never been beyond the park's boundaries since the day they were abandoned. Waggit, on the other hand, had been dumped in the park, captured by rangers, and then rescued from the pound by a woman who adopted him. When she left him at her brother's farm for several months, Waggit mistakenly thought he'd been abandoned again and escaped. Because he had successfully made the hazardous journey back to the park, he was considered a well-traveled animal by the team, and the one most suited to venture into the scary streets beyond the park walls.

His head and shoulders were once again inside a garbage can, and he was trying to get his teeth around some delicious-smelling spare ribs, when he heard a low growl behind him. In his hurry to get out of the trash can and face this unseen threat, he fell back and pulled it on top of him. He lay on the ground, covered in Chinese leftovers and empty soy sauce packets. But this wasn't the worst of his situation, because he was staring into the fierce eyes of the biggest dog he had ever seen, and the dog was not happy.

4

Crossing Boundaries

The dog was enormous, with a dull, matted brown coat; short, stubby ears; a strong, muscled body; and, as far as Waggit could see, no tail at all. But it was his eyes that were his most disturbing feature. There was a black patch over each of them that made it seem like he was wearing a mask. He stared at Waggit with an intensity that made him cower.

"You are in my domain," the big dog said quietly but menacingly. "Why are you here?"

"I apologize," Waggit replied. "I came to get food for my team."

"This is not your team's territory," the big dog continued. "Why isn't there food where you live?"

"The Ruzelas, sir. They're cleaning up the park, and all the prey has gone and we don't know where."

"Ah," said the dog, relaxing a little. "The park. You're a country dog."

Waggit had hated the country when he had been on the farm, but this was not a dog you disagreed with, so he let it pass.

"You hunt your food, am I correct?" the dog asked without waiting for an answer. "It's a repulsive habit, but you've got to survive somehow, I guess. "

"We have to," Waggit replied. "There hasn't been anything in the park to scavenge. That's why they sent me here. We haven't eaten in a long time."

"What is your name, boy?" Despite his civilized tone, the dog's manner was anything but polite. He was threatening and arrogant.

"It's Waggit. My name is Waggit."

"Well, get up, Waggit, and shake yourself off. You're a mess."

Given the other dog's grubby appearance, this criticism surprised Waggit, but he kept this thought to himself and did as he was told.

"My name is Beidel," the other dog said after a moment. "You may have heard of me. I'm the leader of the Ductors. You've heard of them, of course."

Waggit had heard of neither, but he didn't want to admit it to this intimidating dog, so he kept quiet.

"No," continued Beidel, "you don't know who we are, do you? You country dogs lead such isolated lives."

Waggit couldn't allow himself to be called a hick twice.

"Actually," he said quietly but firmly, "we're city dogs who live in the park, which is a whole lot different from the country. I know. I've lived in the country, and believe me it's not the same."

Now it was Beidel's turn to be impressed.

"You've been outside city limits?" he cried. "I never have. How was it?"

"Horrible," Waggit exclaimed with conviction. "But that's because I'm a city dog."

Beidel said nothing, then scratched furiously under his chin and got up and shook himself violently, his huge jowls making slapping sounds as his head rocked from side to side. Dogs do this as a way of clearing their minds.

"What are we going to do with you?" he finally said. "We can't let you scavenge here, but we can't let you starve either."

Waggit was relieved that the solution didn't involve tearing him limb from limb—at least for the moment. There was silence. Waggit watched the other dog carefully, looking for a sudden change of mood that might be a warning sign of an attack. It didn't come. Instead, Beidel made a decision.

"I'm going to give your team this feeder for the time being," he said, "but on one condition. You're going to have to find a solution to your problem that doesn't involve trespassing on my domain."

"But," protested Waggit, "your domain is next to the park, and if we have to go farther out, then the danger gets greater and bringing the food back is more difficult. Besides, if we're not in your domain, we'll be in someone else's, and they'd feel the way you do."

"That's true," agreed Beidel. "If your present situation is unbearable, maybe your team should consider moving. As park dogs you'd be hopeless on the streets, so that's not an option."

Waggit thought about living surrounded by concrete and cars, breathing foul air and dodging the constant threat of humans, and a shudder ran down his spine. To give up the park for that would be even worse than staying without enough food.

"There are other parks," Beidel continued, "that might be better suited to your needs. I've never been in them, of course, but I'm told they're tolerable if you like that sort of thing."

"There probably are," agreed Waggit, "but we don't know where they are or how to get to them."

"We may be able to help you with that," said Beidel. "The Ductors assist dogs in need in various ways, mostly to get them out of the clutches of Uprights. We help them escape, hide them in safe dens, and place them in suitable living arrangements. We usually do it one dog at a time, but I suppose we could move a whole team if necessary. It would certainly be better than having our food stolen."

Waggit sat down and sighed. This was a lot for a young dog to take in. He'd come here only to look for food, and now he was faced with a tough-talking stranger who planned to move the Tazarians out of the park that had always been their home.

"How would we know," he eventually asked, "if the new park was any better than where we are now?"

"That," replied Beidel, "is a gamble you'll have to take. And in the end, what alternative do you have? You either starve where you are or fight us or another street team for a piece of their domain. A fight you'd be unlikely to win."

"It doesn't seem fair," Waggit complained.

"It's not," Beidel assured him. "It never is. Go back to your leader and tell him what I just told you. I will allow you to use this feeder for as many risings as there are claws on one paw, but after that, we will defend it."

Waggit made his way back to the park with a heavy heart. He felt that he'd messed up, but wasn't sure how. Maybe if he'd been more alert, he would have heard Beidel coming and escaped before he got there, not that it would have made any difference. If the big dog hadn't cornered him today, he would have got him the next time. It was inevitable. Waggit's only consolation was that he was returning to the team with a large slab of spare ribs held firmly in his jaws. Even this was hard to enjoy, for he knew that when it was divided up, there would be very little for each team member.

The situation was serious.

When he got back to the team and they had finished off the spare ribs, he nervously told Tazar about his conversation with Beidel.

"No! No! No! We will never leave the park!" Tazar was in a rage. "I don't care what some full-of-himself street hound says. We stay here, and we'll survive. If I'd have been there, I'd have shown him a thing or two."

"But . . . ," Waggit tried to interrupt.

"No buts, Waggit," Tazar snarled. "I'm not blaming you. I'm just angry that a mangy, conniving, no-good mutt would try to take advantage of a naïve young dog who doesn't know better. I tell you, as soon as they moved us out, those—what're they called, Ductors?—would move in here and take over our realm, sure as fleas bite."

Silence fell on the group, and for several minutes the only sound to be heard was Tazar's snorting, for he was still fired up. As usual, Lowdown was the only one brave enough to speak. He cleared his throat.

"While what you say is true, boss," he said, "whether or not these Ductors is villains don't change our predicament. I mean to say, we just finished our meal, and I don't know about you, but I feel as hungry now as before I ate it, and there ain't much of me. Gordo must be thinking someone slit his throat when he wasn't looking."

"Oh no, Lowdown," said Gordo, "I'm sure I'd've noticed if they did that. I am pretty hungry, though."

"I know, I know," Tazar assured them. "It's a bad time. But we've been through bad times before and survived them all. Things will get better. They always do."

But they didn't. Over the next two days there was still no prey to be hunted in the woods, and even with Cal and Raz helping, the amount of food that they could carry from the Chinese restaurant was scarcely enough to live on. And it was getting more and more dangerous. Cal was almost hit by a taxi, and twice a very angry Chinese man chased them off waving a meat cleaver. There wasn't much time; they had to make a decision soon. The period that Beidel would allow them to scavenge in his territory was almost over, and not only was Tazar still adamantly opposed to moving, but they hadn't found an alternative food source either. Waggit turned to Lowdown.

"What are we going to do?" he asked his old friend. "Something's got to happen. We can't go on like this."

"You're right there," agreed Lowdown. "I can't eat any more of that food, for one thing. It makes me all jumpy, and I'm way too old to be jumpy."

"Tazar's never going to agree to the move, is he?" Waggit sighed. "His mind's made up."

"Well," said Lowdown, "you can never tell with Tazar. Something might happen to turn him around."

And indeed it did, but it was nothing that any of them could have anticipated.

5

Rescue and Resolution

The way it happened was like this. The warm spring weather continued, and the park filled up every day with people happy that the bleak days of winter were finally over. This meant there was more wasted food to scavenge, but the visitors still weren't venturing into the Deepwoods, so the dogs continued to travel into the lower reaches of the park to pick up whatever they could find. This wouldn't have been a problem if they could have done it at dusk, when there were fewer people, but one of the features of the new and, at least from a human point of view, improved park management was more frequent trash pickups. Now the window of opportunity to scavenge food from the trash cans was very narrow indeed. But the desperate situation meant that the dogs had to take greater risks in order to supplement the Chinese food, which was rarely enough to feed the whole team.

So it was that Waggit and Magica were making their cautious way from shrub to shrub, staying away from the paths whenever possible. They were looking for trash cans with no humans in the immediate area. Because of the dogs' remarkable sense of smell, they knew which cans had food in them and even what kind it was. They had learned from their previous experience that hiding food anywhere was risky. Once they had retrieved it, they would race back to the pipe as quickly as possible and then return to look for more. All this had to be done with speed, but no matter how fast the two dogs worked, it was still dangerous. Often the crashing sounds that the trash can made as it fell on its side were enough to attract unwanted attention. Because finding and ferrying the food almost the entire length of the park took so much time, they were at risk of capture for longer than usual.

Though this method was less than perfect, it was the best they had come up with, and if you had to do it with anyone, Lady Magica was the dog you would choose. Waggit always loved working with her, whether hunting or foraging. She was fast, smart, and focused. While he enjoyed Cal and Raz as playmates, they were too scattered and prone to making rash decisions. Magica was completely reliable.

They had gone as far as the hill overlooking the lake, where, in days gone by, Lowdown and Waggit used to sit for hours watching the Uprights as they rowed boats across the water. There were no humans nearby, so he and Magica rested for a moment; then she looked around and sighed.

"You know," she said, "it seems to me that there were never this many Uprights around when we lived closer to the Skyline End."

"You're right," Waggit agreed. "There weren't even this many during the hottest rising of the Long Light. If it's like this in the Warming, they'll be bumping into each other later on."

"Well, that'll be worth watching," said Magica, giggling, "as long as they don't bump into us."

Suddenly the two dogs heard a terrified scream.

They looked over and saw that a young child, no more than two or three years old, had fallen from a boat. Her mother, in a desperate attempt to pull her back in, had capsized the rowboat, and now both of them were in the water. The woman was able to keep her head above the surface, but the child was desperate, making muffled crying sounds as she struggled to stay afloat. Without thinking, Waggit leaped to his feet and started running down the hill toward the lake.

"Waggit!" cried Magica. "Stop! Are you crazy?"

Ignoring her, Waggit continued toward the drowning child, leaped into the water, and swam to her. As she disappeared beneath the surface, he managed to catch hold of the back of her dress and bring her spluttering once again into the air. Instinctively he headed toward the bank. It was hard work, because the child continued to thrash about, unaware that he was saving her life.

As he came closer to the bank, he saw another hazard that he hadn't anticipated. A crowd of people had gathered, and some of them had started to wade into the water. At that moment he felt the lake bottom beneath his feet. Realizing that if he could feel it, then she was no longer in danger, he let the child go and started to swim as fast as he could in the opposite direction. Some of the crowd began to run toward him, but he managed to make it to the bank and, without bothering to shake the water from his coat, he ran straight toward the nearest undergrowth. Magica, who had been watching all this in horror, was waiting for him.

"Waggit," she gasped. "That was so stupid. Brave, but really stupid."

"I know," he panted in reply. "I don't know what came over me. I just heard her cries, and I knew I had to try to save her."

"Well, you won't get any thanks from the Uprights," she said, "after the way those ones came after you."

"I didn't do it for thanks," said Waggit somewhat grumpily. He knew he had done a foolish thing and was irritated to have it pointed out.

When they finally returned to the pipe, however, he was warmly grateful to Magica. She described the incident to the other dogs in glowing terms and told of his bravery and skill. Tazar, however, was not impressed.

"That wasn't the smartest thing you ever did," he said calmly. "I know that you had the best intentions, and were obeying a strong instinct, but remember that when you deal with Uprights, your good deed will always be misunderstood. By now they probably think you were the cause of the accident, not the rescuer."

Waggit felt miserable. It was true that some deep, hidden sense had compelled him to dive into the lake and swim after the girl. He realized now that acting instinctively could sometimes get a dog into trouble, and he vowed to think first the next time this happened. He wasn't sure that he could, but he would try.

The situation worsened the following day, when Alona came running into the clearing with a newspaper in her mouth. She laid it on the ground and smoothed it down with her paws. It was the front page of the *New York Post*, most of which was taken up with a photograph of Waggit swimming with the little girl firmly held in his mouth. The headline read: "Mystery Hero Dog Saves Child." Underneath the photograph was a caption that read:

A courageous canine saved three-year-old Amanda
Gerschowitz from a watery death in Central Park
Lake yesterday. The dog ran off before he or his

owner could be thanked by Amanda's sobbing mother. The child's father, famed Wall Street broker Andrew Gerschowitz, has offered a $50,000 reward to the pet's owner.

Unfortunately the dogs couldn't read any of this.

"This is terrible," said Tazar, looking at the photograph. "I knew this would happen."

"What does it mean?" asked Waggit with fear in his voice.

"It means you're a marked dog," Tazar replied. "This is what the Ruzelas do when they target dogs they really want to catch. It's the same as the papers they put on the metal trees."

Tazar was referring to the notices that the distressed owners of lost dogs taped to the lampposts around the park. He was convinced they were like "Wanted" posters and the dogs they depicted were doomed for the Great Unknown.

"Have you seen any more of these?" he asked Alona.

"Oh yes," she replied. "They're all over the place. Everybody's talking about them."

When Alona said everybody, she meant all the

loners. Despite their solitary existence, or maybe because of it, they were the most terrible gossips, and much of the information that Alona got for the team came from this source. It was, however, often unreliable.

"What're we going to do, boss?" Lowdown nervously inquired.

"There's not much we can do," said Tazar, "apart from keeping Waggit away from the Skyline End."

"Well," grumbled Gruff, "I hope he spends the extra time at the Ductors' feeder, since his stupid stunt has cut off food from the Skyline End. Rescuing Uprights! I never heard of such a thing."

"There is one thing we could do," Lowdown suggested.

"What's that?" asked Tazar.

"We could move, like Waggit's friend suggested," said Lowdown.

The dogs gasped at the thought.

"He's not my friend," complained Waggit.

"Whether he is or not ain't the point," said Lowdown. "Although if he could pull this off, he might turn out to be the best friend this team's ever had."

"Do you realize how difficult and dangerous it would

be? It would be hard enough to take a loner from here to another park, never mind all of us," said Tazar.

"Well, I don't mind telling you I ain't moving," screeched Alicia. "You can all go and abandon me, but I'd sooner stay here by myself and do my own hunting."

"Dog, if you think you're skinny now," snorted Cal with laughter, "that ain't nothing like you'd be after a few risings of getting your own prey."

"I ain't skinny," protested Alicia. "I'm slender—there's a difference, not that you'd know."

The Lady Magica brought common sense back to the discussion, as she often did.

"Tazar," she said, "it seems to me that it's none too safe around here anyway, and it's only going to get more difficult the longer we stay here. If this new park lets us live like we used to, wouldn't it be worth getting the danger over in one go rather than have it every day of our lives?"

"If that were the case, my lady," answered Tazar, "then you might be right. The problem is that we don't know what this new park's like. Even the street hound that Waggit's been talking to hasn't been there, and on top of that we don't know what he's like either. There's too much about the whole deal that's unknown."

"There's one way to find out, boss," said Lowdown, "and that's to talk to this dog. See what you think of him. We all know what a good talker you are."

There were some muffled snorts among the team at the last part of this remark. Tazar chose to ignore them.

"I'd talk to anyone who lets us use his feeder," said Gordo, who had suffered most during this time of shortage.

Tazar was silent. The dogs knew that he was having a private conversation in his head. There was no point in interrupting him until it was over.

"I think Gordo's right," he finally said.

Gordo sat up and cocked his head in amazement. It was a phrase he rarely heard.

"The dog," Tazar continued, "was good enough to let us use part of his realm. It was an act of generosity toward brothers and sisters he didn't know, and that alone makes it worthwhile talking to him. Can you arrange a meeting, Waggit?"

"Easily," said Waggit. "This rising's the last claw on my paw. He'll be at the feeder tonight waiting for our answer."

"Then it's settled," said Tazar. "Tonight we will talk."

6

Tazar Meets Beidel

Tazar had decided that he would take Waggit, Cal, and Raz with him to the meeting with Beidel. He would have liked to have the wise advice of Lowdown, but the journey was too difficult for his arthritic limbs. Besides, Tazar had come to rely on Waggit's judgment more and more. Waggit didn't have the experience that the older dog had acquired over many years of life in the park, but he was smart and generally had good instincts. Cal and Raz were included in the party mainly as bodyguards. Both were agile and strong and knew how to handle themselves when in trouble, mostly because they often were.

The dogs had to travel late at night, when there was the least traffic and fewest people on the streets, and while not completely safe, the journey was less dangerous at that hour. Waggit tried to doze beforehand, but he was too wound up. This would be a momentous event in the life of the team, whatever Tazar decided to do. So he lay there with his head on his paws, sighing occasionally for no particular reason. His place for sleeping in the pipe was at the farthest end from the entrance, near where it ran out into a pool of water. He watched the moonlight glitter on the ripples of water caused by the gentle breeze that also ruffled his fur. A spidery pattern of reflections played constantly on the roof of the pipe. It was the perfect place for free dogs to live, he thought, if only people would leave them alone.

Suddenly he heard a low growl.

"Waggit, Cal, Raz, time to move out."

It was Tazar trying to whisper and not disturb the entire team. He needn't have bothered, because everyone was as wound up and awake as Waggit— except for Alicia, who could have slept through a major earthquake in the unlikely event of one hitting New York City. As the four dogs prepared to leave, the others called out "Good luck" and "Safe travels." Even Gruff muttered that they might as well try. He wasn't optimistic about their chances of success but figured that if they got caught, he could have Waggit's spot in the pipe.

As they left the park, they were heartened by the fact that this seemed to be an unusually quiet night. A few yellow taxis trolled for the occasional late-night passenger, and the only other vehicles on the road were newspaper trucks delivering the day's news to stores around the city. They got to the alley behind the Chinese restaurant without incident and were surprised to find that nobody was there. They nervously waited, and leaped to attention several times when a plastic bag was blown along the street and once when a cat scurried past.

"Are you sure you have the same amount of claws on your paw as the rest of us?" Tazar asked Waggit.

"I think so," said Waggit, looking at them. They all compared paws and decided that Waggit's were no different from any other dog's.

Suddenly the hairs on their backs stood up. They

smelled animals approaching, then saw three dogs walking casually down the alley toward them. Beidel was in front, accompanied by two others Waggit had never seen. Beidel walked straight up to Tazar.

"You must be the leader," he said. "What is your name?"

"My name," replied Tazar with the same quiet dignity, "is Tazar, and yours is Beedle, I believe."

"Beidel," said the other. "Rhymes with idle, but that's where the similarity begins and ends."

"I apologize," said Tazar.

"Think nothing of it."

Waggit was getting agitated during this exchange. If it took them this long to establish their names, it would be daylight before any discussions began.

"Allow me to introduce my chief lieutenants," Beidel continued. "This is Dragoman and this is Cicero. Both are skilled in guiding dogs to safety."

The dogs looked as if they were skilled in fighting as well. They carried the scars from past battles, and showed the same quiet self-assurance as their leader. Tazar introduced his three companions, and then they finally got down to the matter at hand.

"I understand from this young dog here," said Beidel, nodding toward Waggit, "that your living situation has become difficult."

"It's the Uprights," growled Tazar. "It's always the Uprights. They cannot tolerate anything they cannot control, and free dogs are intolerable to them."

"It has always been so," said Beidel. "We live among them more than you do, but we have adapted to their ways."

"We have as well, wherever possible," agreed Tazar, "but when their ways take the very food upon which you survive, or when their ways trap you and take you to the Great Unknown, then you cannot adapt. Aside from your generosity in lending us this feeder, we have very little food. Unless we can resolve our problems soon, we will starve."

"Are you willing to consider any other options?" asked Beidel.

"Consider, yes," Tazar answered. "I am a dog of action, but also careful in my actions. I will not expose my team to reckless danger."

"Very noble," said Beidel. "But in these matters there is a level of risk you have to accept. My team has saved many dogs from circumstances far worse than yours, and we can do the same for you if you trust us."

"What is your plan?" Tazar asked.

"Dragoman will explain," Beidel replied.

One of the two lieutenants stepped forward. He was a dog of medium build with a matted black and tan coat. His most noticeable features were his ears, which were long and drooped down either side of his head.

"You are park dogs," he began. "You could no more survive on the streets than we could in the woods. If you can't stay where you are, you have to find another park. We think we know of one that would suit your needs."

"Think?" said Tazar. "I don't like that word. How can we be sure?"

"If certainty is what you demand, then go back to your park and starve," Beidel interrupted irritably. "We have no plans that are based on certainty."

"While we never venture into parks," Dragoman continued, "we know loners who do, and they tell us of one on the far Goldenside near the Wide Flowing Water that sounds right. It is wooded, has many small animals, a couple of feeders, and water. Best of all, it's on a hill and easily defended."

"Are there other teams that live there now?" asked Tazar.

"Not that we know of," replied Dragoman.

"And how would we get there?" asked Tazar. "We are a large team."

The third Ductor, Cicero, stepped forward. He was smaller than Dragoman, with a curly brown coat, and had only one eye, which stared back at them with frightening intensity.

"First of all we will divide you into smaller groups," he said. "We have many safe havens around the city, and a Ductor will take each group to one every rising. We travel only when it is safest, as it is now. During the rising you will sleep, and when the light goes, we travel again."

"How many risings will it take?" asked Tazar.

"Three, maybe four," said Cicero.

Waggit had said nothing at this point, but now he stepped forward beside Tazar.

"One of our members is old," he said, "and it's very hard for him to move. How will he travel such distances?"

"You may have to leave him," said Beidel. " A burden

like that makes the whole group more vulnerable."

"In that case I'll stay with him," Waggit said. "We'll live together in the park the best we can."

"No," Tazar assured him. "Either we all go or none of us do." He turned once more to face Beidel. "Tell me, friend, why would you and your team help us like this? What's in it for you?"

"It's what we do and always have done," Beidel replied. "It's our purpose, and a team with a purpose is a stronger team. Besides which"—he smiled wryly— "it's the only way I can get you to stop stealing our food."

"You've given us much to think about," said Tazar, "and to discuss with the other members of our team. Although I'm their leader and it's my decision, I would not make up my mind without hearing them out. Can we meet again in two risings?"

"No," said Beidel, "I need your decision in one. There are many others in need besides you. If you're not here in one, we withdraw the offer and defend the feeder."

"You're a hard dog, Beidel," said Tazar.

"These are hard times," replied Beidel, and without saying another word, he and his two cohorts disappeared into the night.

Pausing only to gather as much Chinese food as possible, the Tazarians made their way back to the park. They arrived at the clearing by the pipe's entrance just as the first glow of dawn was lighting up the sky.

Even with four dogs carrying all they could, the meal was unsatisfying, and soon they all felt hungry again. Tazar had forbidden any discussion of the meeting until he addressed the group himself. This he did as soon as everyone had finished eating.

"Gather round, gather round," he said, although they already were. He waited until he got their attention, which didn't take long. Then he outlined to them what had happened during the encounter with the Ductors. He explained the plan, its dangers, the possible outcomes, and the reasons for considering such a move in the first place. Waggit was impressed by the way he presented every aspect of the situation clearly and without bias, even though he knew that the leader had strong reservations.

"What it comes down to," Tazar concluded, "is this: Can we continue to live in the Deepwoods, or is it just going to be too hard? And if we have to move, do we trust the Ductors? We have to do this knowing that there will be no going back. As soon as we're out of here another team, probably the Olangsters, will take over our realm. This is forever."

As he finished speaking, an anxious murmur went through the dogs like a long collective growl. They all knew that this was probably the most serious decision any of them would make in their lives. Then the questions started coming, fast and furious.

"How long will we be traveling?"

"Where will we sleep?"

"Are there many Ruzelas in the new park?"

"How do we eat?"

"Will we all be together?"

Tazar noticed that all the questions were about the journey and the new location; none of them focused on what would happen if they stayed where they were. This gave him the answer he had been looking for. The team knew that life in the Deepwoods was about to become intolerable and realized that moving was the only option. It would be tough, but somehow they would do it. His biggest fear was that the new park would be as bad as the situation they were leaving, or worse. Experience had taught him that risk was a constant part of life, especially for free dogs, and his job as a leader was to make sure that the outcome was worth the danger. He instinctively trusted Beidel, and Tazar was a dog who had learned to listen to his instincts.

Waggit was sent at the appointed time to tell the Ductors that the Tazarians agreed to follow their plan. Beidel nodded when he heard their decision. He told Waggit to have the team assembled by the park entrance halfway up the Goldenside on the following night. He also ordered Dragoman and Cicero to take as much food for the Tazarians from the restaurant's trash cans as they could carry, so that the team would start out the journey without completely empty stomachs.

The two Ductors refused to come inside the park but left the food they were carrying just inside the gray stone wall that marked its boundary. Waggit was amazed that animals who seemed as tough and self-assured as these two should be nervous of trees and grass, until he remembered how edgy Cal and Raz had been on the city's streets. He said good-bye to the

Ductors and told them he looked forward to seeing them the next day, though this was an exaggeration. While he thought that the move was the right thing to do, the journey wasn't something he was looking forward to.

7

The Sad Farewell

The following night the team assembled behind some large rhododendron bushes near the entrance to the park, where they had arranged to meet the Ductors. They remained hidden because Tazar was still wary. He believed Beidel was trustworthy, but he was not too proud to realize he might be wrong. There was no reason to take chances if you didn't have to.

The weather had become hot and humid, and they could hear the low rumble of thunder, as if the elements disapproved of the journey they were about to take. The electricity the storm generated made their coats tingle and prickle, increasing the nervousness and discomfort that they were feeling. Even Tazar had been known to flinch when a flash of lightning came close. Of all the dogs, only Gordo was unaffected by thunderstorms. Alicia was sure this was due to his lack of breeding, although he was no less well bred than any of the others.

This was a difficult time for all of them, and not just because of the hazards they would face. Except for Waggit, even those who weren't born there had never been outside the park after they were first abandoned. They knew that this would be the last time they would see the place that had been their home for as long as they could remember, and they felt a deep sadness at saying good-bye.

Four dogs approached the park entrance: Dragoman, Cicero, and two others they hadn't seen before. One, a female, had a loping stride that indicated a German shepherd was somewhere in her family tree. The other was a medium-size dog with a wiry coat that looked as if a hurricane had just blown through where he was standing. His fur stood up at a variety of different angles, which would have been funny if not for his stern appearance. This dog was all business: alert, focused, and tense. The Tazarians held their breath, waiting to see what the Ductors would do. The wirehaired dog lifted his head, his nose twitching in the air. He said something to his companions that the Tazarians couldn't hear, and then the four of them approached the bushes that concealed the team.

When Tazar realized their hiding place had been discovered, he emerged from it, with the rest of the team behind him. Dragoman nodded to him in greeting.

"You're cautious," he said. "I like that. It's a quality that will come in handy before this journey's over."

"And beyond," Tazar assured him.

"Beyond's none of my business," Dragoman said. "I'll take care of the journey; and that," he continued, looking around the team, "is more than enough for me. We never moved this many dogs before."

"They're good dogs," said Tazar. "Smart and sensible. They learn quickly too. They won't give you any trouble."

Dragoman glanced at Gordo and Alicia. "Smart" and "No trouble" weren't the first words that sprang to his mind, and he wondered how many of the other team members were unworthy of Tazar's glowing recommendation. He knew he would find out soon enough.

"These are your guides," he said, nodding toward the two unfamiliar dogs. "This is Naviga and this Pilodus. They will lead you to your safe havens. Cicero and I will bring up the rear of each group."

"*One* group," snarled Tazar. "There is only one group. We travel together or not at all. Where is Beidel?"

"Beidel never comes on missions," Cicero answered. "You *may* see him at one of the havens, but you're in our paws now, and you must trust us. We know what we're doing, and what we're doing is breaking you up into two groups. It will be dangerous enough even then, and the first havens are too small to take all of you together."

"I don't like the idea of being separated," Tazar complained.

"It's the best way," Dragoman assured him, "and we are still in your park. If you wish to change your mind, now is the time. Once we're on the streets, it'll be too late."

"No," said Tazar, "there's no going back. But if

any harm comes to this team, you'll have to answer to me."

"Remember, friend," Dragoman said, quietly but firmly, "we do this for your advantage, not our own."

And so Tazar and Waggit divided up the team. All the dogs assumed that Lowdown would go with Waggit. Magica decided to join them, and wherever she went, so did Little One and Little Two, not to mention Gordo, who would be miserable without her. Cal and Raz decided to go with Tazar, as did Alicia, who was under the misguided notion that she could twist him around her little claw. That left Gruff and Alona. Gruff said that since they were all going to be captured or killed in traffic, it didn't matter to him which group he died with, and Alona would never be so bold as to state her preference. In the end Gruff went with Tazar's group and Alona stayed with Waggit.

Before they went their separate ways, Tazar assembled the dogs.

"Listen up," he commanded. "We all know how difficult this is going to be, but if we do as our guides tell us, and with luck on our side, we'll make it. But if for any reason I don't, Waggit becomes the team leader.

He's a fine dog, and I've taught him all I know. Now, I expect to be with you in our new home, but you never know what will happen. There's only one thing I ask of you: If you have to go on without me, keep the name Tazarians. The Waggits just doesn't have the same ring to it."

There was a stunned silence. Nobody in the team had ever conceived of Tazar not being there. Waggit was especially taken aback; it was the first time the leader had officially declared him his successor. Cicero broke the hush.

"We must be on our way. We have to reach the havens before first light."

The newly formed groups said their good-byes, brushing against each other and licking muzzles. Then they moved out, each headed in opposite directions— Tazar's to the south and Waggit's to the north. Pilodus led Waggit's dogs, with Cicero in the rear. Since the job of the last dog was to act as security against any danger that might creep up from behind, Waggit was nervous about having a one-eyed dog in that role.

They moved slowly and silently, using the parked vehicles that lined the sidewalks as cover. It was the closest most of them had ever been to cars, so they were cautious and on edge. At this time of night the city had a strange, peaceful beauty. There was little traffic, and even fewer people. They had covered two blocks before they saw anyone. Their one encounter was with a young couple so obviously in love that they only had eyes for each other, and remained blissfully unaware that nine dogs lay hidden under the cars they passed. The buildings were elegant town houses, some with columns flanking the front doors at the top of wide steps. When the dogs came to the end of a block and had to negotiate a broad avenue, Pilodus would cross first and wait on the opposite corner. When it was safe to go, he would let out a soft "Yip" and one of the waiting dogs would then run over to him and quickly hide under a car. This was repeated until every dog was on the other side, and only then would they move forward.

After a few blocks Pilodus stopped at an intersection with an avenue that was different from the others. Normally the avenues ran at right angles to the cross streets, but this one went diagonally. It was wider and had a dividing strip in the middle planted with some bedraggled-looking flowers. Instead of immediately ushering the dogs across, Pilodus assembled them in the front yard of a house and addressed them.

"Okay, here's the thing," he said. "We gotta go on the updown now, and that's the most dangerous part of the journey tonight, 'cause there ain't much cover. The Uprights don't let their rollers sleep on updowns like they do on the crossovers."

"What's an updown?" inquired Magica.

"It's a road that goes either up or down, depending on which way you go on it," replied Pilodus. "Now we can either take the divider or the walking part. The divider's a bit safer because it's farther away from the Uprights, but it's also more dangerous on account of being closer to the rollers. The walking part's the opposite, but it does have the advantage of a few sleeping rollers for cover."

"Are you saying we should choose?" asked Waggit.

"You're the ones most at risk," Cicero intervened. "If any dog gets caught, it'll likely be one of you, not Pilodus or me. So you decide where you'd be most comfortable."

Waggit looked at the center of the road and then at Lowdown. The old dog had been trying to keep up, but it was obvious that he was in a lot of pain and was beginning to limp badly. Scrambling up and down on the raised beds that formed the divider would be hard on his short legs even without the stiffness and pain of his arthritis.

"We'll take the walking part," Waggit said, without bothering to consult with the others, all of whom seemed perfectly happy to let him take charge.

"Fine with me," said Pilodus. "The flowers on the divider make me sneeze anyway. Here's how we do it. We spread out with big gaps between dogs. That way if you're spotted, it looks like you're by yourself. Uprights won't bother about one free dog, but if they see all of us together, that's another matter. If you catch sight of an Upright, either hide under a sleeping roller, or walk, don't run, past them—and whatever you do, *don't look at them.* If they try to grab you, just run as fast as you can, and we'll send out searchers to find you!"

All this sounded like their worst nightmare come true, and more than one of them considered turning around and hightailing it back to the park. Waggit sensed this and knew he had to say something.

"We can do it" was the best he could come up with.

Somewhat despondently they set off. Pilodus went first, keeping close to the curb, moving briskly but casually until he was halfway up the block. At this point Magica set out, and then Gordo, who waited until she got to the same place before he left. Watching Gordo lumber along trying to look inconspicuous would have been hilarious under less serious circumstances. Then Little One and Little Two left together. Although Pilodus had told everybody to go one by one, Little One and Little Two were so inseparable that it never occurred to them to follow this command.

Waggit could see the reason for spreading out, but he was worried that the distance between the lead dog and the tail end would be so great that they would be unable to communicate with each other should something happen. He was just about to express this fear to Cicero when their luck changed. The storms that had been threatening ever since they'd left the park suddenly broke, and torrential rain began to pour down on them. It was so heavy that you could barely see a paw in front of your face. The few cars and taxis on the road crawled almost to a halt. The raindrops came down so fast and heavy that they stung the dogs' eyes and drenched their coats. It was the perfect weather for a group of stray dogs to pass unnoticed through the streets of New York.

Cicero reacted first.

"Come on, let's go!" he yelled. "Bunch up and run."

And run they did, water streaming off the ends of their ears and tails. They ran block after block until suddenly Pilodus and the rain stopped, almost at the same time.

"This way," he told the panting dogs. "We need to cut across here."

They quickly ran to the other side of the wide and scary road that they had just navigated, eager to head down the quieter and safer cross streets. But there was one problem. Lowdown was nowhere to be seen.

8

The First Haven

Waggit was the first to notice his absence.

"Lowdown's not here. Has anyone seen him?"

The dogs hadn't seen much of anything during the storm; they had been preoccupied with staying together in the blinding rain. Now they looked around, startled to realize that the old dog wasn't with them.

"Oh no," said Magica. "This is terrible. Where can he be?"

"You talking about the old guy with the short legs?" asked Cicero. "I passed him way back there.

He wasn't keeping up at all."

"Why didn't you stop to help him?" demanded Waggit, angry that his friend had been left to fend for himself.

"Because that would have put everyone in danger," Cicero replied. "This way only one dog is in trouble."

"We gotta go," Pilodus interrupted. "If we don't leave now, we won't get to the haven before light. Let's get to safety and then we'll send out searchers."

"No," said Waggit. "I'm going back for him."

"We'll wait for you," Gordo assured him. "Either we all go together or none of us do."

As much as he hated to admit it, Waggit knew that Cicero was right—you couldn't put the whole team in danger for the sake of one dog, no matter how loved that dog was.

"No," he said. "You guys go on. There's nothing you could do but hang around here waiting. You might as well do that in a safe place, and this street corner isn't it. I'll go back and find Lowdown and get him to the haven."

"But you don't know where it is," said Magica.

"Okay, this is what we do," said Pilodus, who was clearly getting worried about the time. "Waggit, take a good look at this corner and really try to remember it, 'cause many of them look alike 'round here. What you do when you get back here with the other dog is head down this crossway in the direction away from the park. Keep going for a few blocks, and we'll have eyes and ears looking out for you. The haven's straight down this street."

Waggit looked around. On one corner was a bank, and on another was a shoe store. The third corner had a twenty-four-hour delicatessen, and under its awning an employee was tilted back on a chair, fast asleep. The most conspicuous building was a movie theater, with a brightly lit marquee and sparkling lights, about a third of the way up the block on the side where they were standing. Waggit had no idea what a movie theater was, but he knew that he would remember its glitter.

Reassuring the Tazarians that he would catch up with them soon, he went back the way they had come. He hung close to the few parked vehicles, knowing that his wily friend would use them for cover if he was resting his aching limbs. Already there were more people on the streets, even though the dawn had not yet broken, and Waggit worried about the journey they would have to take to get back to the others.

He had gone only three blocks when he suddenly stopped, shocked by what he saw. There was
Lowdown, lying in the middle of the sidewalk, making
no attempt to hide. As Waggit watched, a pedestrian
passed right by, staring at the forlorn-looking old dog
with his scruffy coat. Waggit quickly ran up to him.

"Lowdown, are you crazy?" he yelped. "You've got
to get away from here."

His friend looked up at him with a mournful look
in his brown eyes.

"I can't, Waggit," he said. "It hurts too much. I
must've been crazy to think I could make a journey
like this. This is only the beginning, and I'm already
finished. You go back to the others; they need you.
I'm just going to lie here until the Ruzelas get me, and
then whatever happens, happens."

"No," said Waggit. "I won't let you. I need you too
much. You're coming back with me."

And without saying another word he picked up
Lowdown in his mouth, grabbing him by the loose
skin at the back of the neck, and ran across the road
to the divider, carrying the struggling old dog like a
mother would hold a puppy.

"Hey, hey, what're you doing?" Lowdown protested.

"Put me down! Ouch, ow, that hurts! You're worse than the Ruzelas, and I ain't kidding."

By this time they were on a patch of grass in the divider. Although it wasn't as soft as the soil in the park, it was still more forgiving than the sidewalk. Waggit lowered Lowdown onto it.

"Ugh," Waggit said, spitting bits of Lowdown's coat out of his mouth, "your fur tastes awful."

"Well," replied Lowdown, "it ain't there for you to eat! So now what're we gonna do?"

"We're going to take it very slowly up the center here until we get to where we turn off, and then we're going to join the others in the haven. They told me it's not far from here."

"And if I don't wanna go?" asked Lowdown.

"Then my teeth go around the back of your neck," Waggit replied.

"You know, I'm sure glad you're my friend," said Lowdown. "I can't imagine what you'd be like if you was my enemy!"

Despite Lowdown's protests, Waggit's rescue mission seemed to have renewed the old dog's energy and spirit. They headed north along the divider, with Waggit in the lead. Every so often he would look over his shoulder, and it upset him to see his friend limping along slowly and painfully. Although they were making progress, so was the dawn. As the sky lightened, the traffic increased. Every time the dogs came to an intersection, they faced an even harder problem. Lowdown was too weak to jump down from the divider, cross the street, and then hop back up, so after each block Waggit had to pick him up in his mouth and transport him the short distance to the next section.

In this manner they gradually made their way uptown. Although Lowdown's body hadn't improved, his spirits had. Waggit glanced over his shoulder again and was glad to see how much happier he seemed. But then something else caught his eye. It was the front of the movie theater, not sparkling as much now in the daylight, but the same one for sure, and now more than a block behind them.

"Stupid, stupid, stupid," Waggit said.

"You or me?" asked Lowdown.

"Me," Waggit replied. "I was concentrating on where *you* were and I lost track of where *I* was. We've gone past the place where we have to turn."

"Oh well," said Lowdown, cheerfully, "I hear that

walking's good for you—keeps you young, or so they say."

As they turned to go back, Waggit suddenly saw the familiar sight of a blue and white police car coming toward them as it drove downtown.

"Ruzelas," he warned. "Down."

This warning applied more to Waggit than it did to Lowdown, who was pretty much "down" all the time. The difference between him standing and lying flat out was no more than an inch or two. The two dogs lay partially hidden by some bedraggled daisies. The car drew close and stopped at the traffic light. They held their breath. Luckily the officer in the passenger seat was on his cell phone, and the driver was looking up at the light, waiting for it to change. Finally it did and they left.

"Phew," said Waggit. "That was close. Let's get to the crossover as quickly as we can."

As quickly as they could was still pretty slow, but they finally made it, and started going in what they hoped was the direction of the haven. Suddenly Lowdown let out a yelp of pain. Waggit turned to see him standing on three legs, holding one off the ground, with a grimace of pain across his face.

"Waggit," he said, "I can't go on. I gotta rest."

"Okay, old pal," said Waggit reassuringly. "We'll stop here for a while under this car—let you catch your breath and rest your leg."

Waggit noticed that all the cars were parked on the opposite side of the street. Why this was he had no idea, but there was a solitary vehicle on their side that they crawled underneath; and they settled down for a rest. Even Waggit was feeling tired, especially after having stayed up all night coupled with the stress of the journey. They were just contemplating a nap when the roar of a diesel engine rattled the air. A truck pulled up in front of their hiding place. They heard its door open and shut and then saw the feet of its driver approach them. He paused, and suddenly his face appeared by the front wheels. Fortunately the two dogs were resting up against the rear tires, and he seemed too preoccupied to notice them. He looked around at the front end of the vehicle and then went back to the truck. The dogs had no alternative but to stay where they were and see what happened. There was a roar from the truck's engine, a clanging of metal, and the sound of chains being dragged across the pavement. Then to their surprise the front of their hiding place rose up, and the whole vehicle lurched forward, leaving them unprotected and under the full gaze of a traffic cop.

"Hey! What the . . . ?" she yelled at them. "Get away from here."

Although they didn't understand a word she was saying, they did as they were told. Lowdown hobbled along on three legs, with Waggit behind him, making sure they weren't being chased. Far ahead of them their former shelter was being towed to a pound, but not one for dogs.

When they had put enough distance between them and the traffic cop, Lowdown stopped, panting so violently that his whole body shook.

"I'm beginning to wonder," he gasped, "whether I would've been better off waiting for the Ruzelas to get me. The Great Unknown can't be worse than this."

"It is," said Waggit, who had been there. "Trust me on this one."

When they had both regained their breath, they continued at a more leisurely pace. The neighborhood they were passing through was less well kept than the blocks near the park, and there were more people on the streets. These people didn't seem bothered by two stray dogs wandering by, and sometimes greeted them with "Hey, doggie, doggie," and "Here, boy," which Lowdown and Waggit deliberately ignored.

They soon approached a vacant lot between two houses. A chain-link fence sealed off the empty space, and the lower part of the enclosure was covered in frayed black tarpaulin. The two dogs had almost passed the lot when they heard a soft "Yip." They turned around but couldn't see where the voice was coming from. Then they noticed that one corner of the fence had been bent back, and through it they could barely make out the figure of a dog on the other side.

"Hey, you!" he cried.

"Us?" asked Waggit.

"Yeah, you," said the dog. "Are you Wiggy and Liedown?"

"Close enough"—Lowdown chuckled—"don't you think, Wiggy?"

But "Wiggy" was being serious.

"Who wants to know?" he asked.

"S'okay," said the other dog, "I'm your receptor. They told me to look out for you."

"You're our what?" asked Waggit.

"Your receptor," said the dog. "I'm in charge here."

"In charge of what?" Waggit was still confused.

"The haven. You've arrived. Come and join the others."

The dog used his stocky body to push the fence aside, and Lowdown and Waggit cautiously went through the gap he made. Waggit was worried that this might be a trap. Lowdown was too tired and in too much pain to worry about anything. Once they were on the other side of the fence, they looked around and were depressed by what they saw. The area was strewn with trash and large boxes that had once contained appliances. Weeds grew everywhere, and the whole place smelled of decay. For two dogs used to the fresh smells of the park, this was the city at its worst.

"*This* is *it?*" asked Waggit in disgust. "*This* is the haven?"

"Yup," said the receptor proudly. "Neat, ain't it? You'd never know it was here, would you?"

"But nothing's here," said Waggit. "Just a load of old boxes."

"Ah, that's the point," said the receptor. "Come on in."

He then led them to the far corner of the lot, where the walls of two adjacent buildings came together. A pile of the boxes lay against them, and the receptor disappeared through the open end of one. Waggit and Lowdown followed. What they saw next was a surprise, to say the least. From the outside what looked like many cartons was in fact one large space when you went in. They had been artfully positioned together, with pieces chewed out of their sides to create an area just large enough to hide five Tazarians and two Ductors, all of whom were sleeping.

9

Lowdown's Limo

Magica was the first to wake up.

"Waggit. Thank Vinda you're both safe!"

"Is everyone else okay?" Waggit inquired.

"Oh yes," she replied, "we're all fine, especially now you two are back. It's not great here, but it will do for now."

"Not great" was Magica's way of dealing with a situation that was close to intolerable. The dogs lay packed together in the tight space, where the heat was stifling and the smell overpowering.

"How's Lowdown?" she whispered.

"Not in good shape," Waggit replied. "He's in a lot of pain, and I don't think he'll make it all the way unless we do something."

"What *can* we do?" she asked.

"I haven't a clue at the moment," Waggit said.

Gordo rolled over, causing Little Two to growl as the large dog's body squashed him. Gordo opened one bleary eye.

"Waggit! Hi!" he said. "Where's Lowdown?"

"Right next to you, and already in the land of dreams."

Exhausted by the journey and his discomfort, the old dog had curled up in what little space was left and fallen asleep instantly. Waggit decided to join him, even though his own rear end was sticking partway out of the box. The receptor, whose name nobody seemed to know, kept watch outside.

Waggit woke up several hours later, cramped and hot. Apparently he wasn't the only dog feeling that way—the sound of panting tongues was almost deafening. It wasn't dark yet, but soon would be. The sounds of the summer evening filled the still, moist air. People were sitting on balconies and fire escapes, or congregating in the street beyond the wire fence. Loud music and the smell of barbecue drifted into the boxes where the dogs lay hidden.

"Why are we all still in here?" asked Waggit. "Why don't we go outside, where it must be cooler?"

"Because Cicero and Pilodus told us not to," replied the ever-obedient Gordo.

"Did they say why?" Waggit asked impatiently.

"They said that some of the Uprights who live in the buildings can look into this area, and if they saw all of us milling around here, they would get the Ruzelas," Magica explained. "They said it would be better if we wait until it's completely dark before coming out."

"And this rule doesn't apply to them? We have to do as they say, like always," growled Waggit grumpily. Neither Ductor was around.

"No," said Alona, "they went off to their stash to get some food for us. I hope they're okay. It's pretty risky out in the open at this time of the darkening, 'specially if you're dragging back food."

When he listened to Alona, Waggit realized two things—first how hungry he was and second how ashamed he was of his outburst. He decided that one must have caused the other, but even so, he was embarrassed at having reacted so immaturely.

"I wish they'd hurry up," Little One chimed in. "I'm starving."

Waggit turned around and cautiously stuck his head out of the box. He looked around for the receptor but couldn't see him at first. Then there was a movement in a clump of ragweed close to the boxes.

"You're awake, I see" came the voice of the receptor. "How did you sleep?"

"Uncomfortably," replied Waggit, "but well enough under the circumstances."

"I apologize," said the receptor. "The trouble is that when we built this haven, we never thought we'd have to house so many dogs. We thought one or two would be the most at any one time."

"I understand," said Waggit. "It's good of you to help us in this way."

"It is, isn't it?" said the receptor. "I honestly don't know why we do it sometimes. We hardly ever get any thanks. Still, it passes the time, I suppose. Better than just hanging around getting on each other's nerves."

"Where are Cicero and Pilodus?" asked Waggit.

"They'll be back soon," replied the receptor. "They've already made two runs to the stash, and they still had to go back for more. That's another thing we never thought we'd have to do—feed so many dogs."

The longer the conversation went on, the worse Waggit felt. It also occurred to him that if anything happened to the two Ductors while they were getting the food, he and his group would be stuck. They had no idea where the new park was, or how to get there. The thought made him very nervous.

He was thoroughly relieved, then, when he saw Cicero and Pilodus return, one of them carrying a slab of spare ribs. Waggit wondered whether he would have to eat spare ribs for the rest of his life. Until recently he'd never had one; now that was all he seemed to consume. They were tasty, but they did prove that sometimes you could have too much of a good thing.

As soon as they considered it dark enough for the Tazarians to leave the boxes, the Ductors assembled all the food they had brought and divided it up among their guests. They insisted that they had eaten at the stash, and this was all for the Tazarians and the receptor. The meal was the usual strange mix of city food that the dogs had now become used to. Waggit was surprised at how much he missed freshly killed meat, especially because he had been so reluctant to hunt when he was younger.

After they had finished the meal, their guides suggested that they rest until it was quiet enough for them
to move out. Waggit found it difficult to relax. He was
on edge, thinking about Lowdown and worried about
how he would handle the next part of the journey.

"How are you feeling?" he asked the old dog.

"Oh, not so bad," Lowdown replied. "I ain't exactly
raring to go, but I feel a lot better than I did."

Gradually the noise from the streets calmed down,
and finally the silence they had been waiting for settled all around them. Cicero and Pilodus decided it
was time to move out, and the dogs prepared to leave.
Waggit made sure that each of them said good-bye
and thank you to the receptor as he held back the wire
fence to let them out onto the street. They headed in
the same direction as the previous night. They hadn't
gone more than a block before it became obvious that
Lowdown was in trouble again. He limped badly and
could move at only the slowest pace. Cicero gathered
them into an empty parking lot to discuss the situation.

"We've gotta make better time than this," he said.
"Not only is it dangerous to move so slowly, but we

also have other dogs waiting for our help, and unless we get you to the new park quickly, we won't be able to help them."

"I can't go any faster than I am," Lowdown said.

"In that case," said the Ductor, "we'll have to leave you to make your own way as best you can."

This caused a wave of growls and rumblings among the Tazarians.

"You know," said Lowdown wearily, "before Waggit came back to fetch me after the rainstorm, I'd given up. I was in such pain, and the journey was so hard that it didn't seem worth going on. But when I saw Waggit's face and I realized how worried he was and how much he cared for me, then I thought 'I'm as much a part of this team as any dog.' Actually I think I was around before there *was* a team. I realized that I want to see our new home, and if I'm going to die—*when* I die—I want to do it surrounded by dogs who love me and I love back." He paused for a second. "If there's any way you can get me to the new park, please help me go there."

They were so moved by Lowdown's plea, they couldn't speak.

"If I stayed with Lowdown, how would we find

the next haven?" Waggit asked Pilodus after a few moments.

"It's not hard," he replied. "You just keep going on this street until you can't go any farther and then turn uptown. That'll bring you there. Once we've got these dogs settled, Cicero and I can come back to help you find it."

"Let's do it," said Waggit. "You guys take off and we'll follow—slowly maybe, but we'll get there."

The dogs all agreed that this was the best solution, and soon Waggit and Lowdown were by themselves.

"I wish I wasn't such a burden," Lowdown said after they had walked in silence for a while. "Getting old is no fun, let me tell you. If it wasn't for the alternative, I wouldn't recommend it."

"I'll be thankful if I grow old enough to be a burden," Waggit replied. "A lot of us don't. Did I ever tell you about the dog next to me in the Great Unknown?" Waggit had spent only a short period of his life in the dog pound before being rescued, but he had never forgotten it. "He was a really nice dog, but he didn't make it. I sometimes wonder how any of us do."

It was in this somber frame of mind that they slowly continued down the street, stopping frequently for Lowdown to catch his breath and rest his legs. As on the previous night, there were very few people about, but Waggit also worried about meeting other dogs who were not members of the Ductors. He was sure that they were probably on someone else's territory, and that the owners would defend it fiercely if they spotted intruders. Because of this fear he pushed Lowdown under a parked car when he saw two dogs in the distance running toward them. It wasn't until the animals were quite close that he realized they were Little One and Little Two, and that Little One had something in his mouth, and a very large something at that.

As Little One got closer, Waggit could see that it was a flat board with wheels attached to it. One end was badly broken, as if it had smashed into something with great force.

"Look what we found" cried Little Two, when they finally got to where Waggit and Lowdown were standing. "It may be the answer to Lowdown's problems."

"It may be," said Lowdown, "if only we knew what it was."

"Well," asked Waggit, "what is it?"

"Dunno," Little Two replied, "but it's very cool. Little One can't put it down because it runs away."

"How can it run away?" asked Waggit. "I mean, it's not like it's an animal or anything."

"Show him, Little One," ordered Little Two.

His friend put the thing down on its wheels and released it from his jaws. Immediately it started rolling down the slope of the road away from them.

"See," said Little Two gleefully, and pounced on it before it went too far. This had obviously been the source of several games before the two fun-loving dogs had had the idea that it could be used to transport Lowdown.

"The only way to stop it," continued Little Two, Little One's mouth being full again, "is to lay it on its back with its legs in the air. But if you turned it the right way up and put Lowdown on it, we could pull him along and all he would have to do is stand there. Going downhill we wouldn't even have to pull."

"You think?" said Waggit, looking suspiciously at the broken skateboard.

"No," interrupted Lowdown. "They don't think. They're nuts, the pair of them. There's no way I'm getting on that thing, whatever it is."

"That's the trouble with old dogs," said Little Two. "They never want to try anything new."

"Wrong," Lowdown corrected him. "The trouble with old dogs is they want to become older dogs, and they ain't gonna achieve that by going along with your hopper-brained schemes."

"But you know," said Waggit, "if it worked, it would mean we could keep up with the others, and you wouldn't be in any pain."

"No," Lowdown insisted.

"Please," begged Waggit. "Just try it."

Lowdown sighed.

"I always suspected insanity was catching," he said resignedly. "I'll try it just once, but I ain't making any promises."

So with Little One steadying the board in his mouth, Lowdown gingerly climbed onto it. His legs were so short that even this was difficult. He stood on his new perch and looked around.

"I feel ridiculous up here."

Little One was about to mention that anything that made Lowdown taller was a good thing when he let go of the board. It immediately shot out from under the small dog, throwing Lowdown to the ground with a crash.

"Ow! Ow! Ow!" he yelled. "I thought you said I

wasn't going to be in any pain."

It took several minutes of persuasion, plus a solemn promise from Little One never to let go of the board again, before Lowdown would agree to get back on. Finally the old dog got the hang of staying on it.

"You see," said Little Two, "you just needed to get your balance"

"It ain't me that's unbalanced," growled Lowdown. "It's you two's brains."

They moved forward at a brisk pace, Little One pulling and Little Two steering from the back. Waggit was worried about the amount of noise the wheels were making, so he was the lookout. After a while it became obvious that Lowdown was thoroughly enjoying himself.

"You know," he said, chuckling, "this turned out to be not such a bad idea after all."

The road began to slope down at this point, and Little One, whose neck was getting stiff, released the board.

"You can go by yourself for a bit," he said.

"Whoa," yelled Lowdown as he began to gather speed. But then he discovered that if he put his weight on one side or the other, he could actually steer the board. What he didn't know was how to stop it. Luckily there was a corner store at the bottom of the hill whose owners had put out a pile of cardboard boxes for the trash collectors. Lowdown, realizing that they were the softest option open to him, steered toward them and hit them with a thump.

Despite a good deal of complaining about the stupidity of making something that you couldn't stop, Lowdown had enjoyed the whole experience enough to get back on. He insisted that at least one set of dog jaws hold the skateboard at all times, downhill as well as up. This time Little One kept his promise, and the four dogs made their way, noisily, in the direction of their teammates.

10

The Return of a Friend

The slope that had caused Lowdown's collision with the boxes now got steeper, and it took all of Little One and Little Two's strength to keep the skateboard from running away with its passenger. The road went under a highway that had traffic rumbling over it, even at this time of night. When they came to the other side of the underpass, they faced another broad avenue, and on the far side Waggit spotted a park. His heart leaped for joy at the sight of trees, bushes and grass. Even though this was only the second night of their journey, he longed for the feel and smell of earth and leaves, and to walk on something softer than concrete. Could this be the new park? he wondered optimistically. Then he remembered that Cicero told them they would stay in at least one more haven before reaching their destination. But maybe if this one met their needs, they wouldn't have to travel so far. The Ductors had admitted they knew little of parks.

The three dogs hurriedly pushed and pulled Lowdown across the street, and had just entered the park's confines when they met up with Pilodus and Cicero. Even the stern-faced Cicero allowed himself a grin when he saw Lowdown on his skateboard. The old dog tried to maintain as much dignity as possible, and stood upright like an emperor in his chariot.

"That's pretty neat," said Pilodus.

"Yeah," Waggit replied. "Neat but noisy."

"That won't matter," the other dog assured him. "We don't go on any more streets to get to the haven. Make as much noise as you like."

"Would this park be a possibility for us?" inquired Waggit. "Is there anything wrong with it?"

"In a word, Stoners and Skurdies," said Pilodus, although of course these were three words. "The

Skurdies ain't so bad if you leave them alone, but Stoners . . . well, you must know about Stoners."

The park dogs knew far too much about Stoners, especially in the Deepwoods, where many of them hung out. They were gangs of young men, bored and ready to harass anything that lived there. They mostly tormented homeless people, known to the dogs as Skurdies, or the dogs themselves, especially loners. They were called Stoners because rocks were their favorite weapons, but sometimes they also carried knives, and they had been known to kill animals with them. They were a very good reason not to live here.

"Oh well," said Waggit, "I guess we have to keep on going, then. How far is the haven from here?"

"It's not far," said Cicero. "The others are already settled in for the night. We'll get there soon."

They followed a narrow paved footpath that wound down a hill. To make things easier, Lowdown got off the skateboard and walked while Little One carried it in his mouth. None of the Tazarians were prepared for what happened next. When they came to the crest of the hill, they were met with a sight that took their breath away. It was a river, bigger than anything any of them had ever seen. The moonlight reflected off its surface, making it look like polished steel, and on its far bank thousands of lights twinkled, as if it wore a jeweled crown. It was so monumental and magnificent that none of the dogs could speak, and Little One dropped the skateboard with a clatter as his jaw fell open. The streams in the park were nothing compared to this. Waggit, during his adventures in the world outside, had seen rivers, but even the biggest one was just a dribble compared to this awesome expanse of water.

"What," he asked in a hushed voice, "is that?"

"That?" replied Pilodus in a matter-of-fact voice. "Oh, that's the Wide Flowing Water. It's evil."

"How can something so beautiful be evil?" asked Little Two.

"It's not like any other water," said Pilodus. "It has a force that lives within it and sucks you down and drags you many realms away. Whatever you do, never swim in it. Dogs have tried, but none ever returned. Don't even drink it. If you do, you'll go mad."

Pilodus's warning sounded terrifying. Lowdown tried to change the subject.

"What's on the other side?" he asked, looking at the sparkling lights on the opposite bank.

"Those are the Far Distant Territories. Nobody we know has ever been there, and nobody probably ever will," answered Pilodus. Without another word he took the path that headed north. The dogs followed him, with Lowdown back on his board, watching the majestic river and the looming black barges. The park now narrowed to the point where it was really only the path they were on, with the river on their left and the highway to the right. The dogs stayed on the paved path for some time until it suddenly ended.

A short distance in front of them was the wall of a large building that jutted out over the water on thick concrete columns. A vague rumbling hum of machinery could be heard from within. Where the sidewalk ended, a path veered off to its left over the grassy embankment in the direction of the overhanging construction. If you were a human being, you would never have known of its existence, but the dogs could smell the presence of others who had passed along it. It ran toward the river, but just before reaching the water, it ascended steeply over some rocks and under the canopy of the building. The dogs scrambled up, and where it flattened out, they came upon a huge area completely covered and sheltered from the weather.

Here they found the rest of their group happily tucked away, either snoozing or grooming.

This haven was a major improvement over the previous night's shelter. It was immense, running the full length of the building, and could have held twenty times their team with room to spare. The trash cans of the adjacent park held a convenient and, at this time of year, constant supply of food, so much that the Ductors didn't even bother to have a stash but would just forage every evening for their dinner. In fact the other Tazarians had already eaten, but the haven's receptor, a shy female with whom Alona had already bonded, assured them that she had saved them a meal.

Clear water ran from a pipe that stuck out of the ground, and Waggit, who was feeling ferociously thirsty, went up and sniffed it.

"It's okay," said the receptor in a soft voice. "It's perfectly safe to drink."

The first haven's drinking arrangements had consisted of an old white plastic bucket that caught the rain. Even though the storm that night had filled it up, the water still tasted funny and had a chemical tang to it. Waggit cheerfully stuck his snout into the stream coming out of the pipe; but he underestimated the force of it and nearly drowned without ever going near the Wide Flowing Water. He spluttered and sneezed and shook his head.

"Oh no," sympathized the receptor. "I should have told you about that. You have to be very careful and just drink from the edges. It's also easier if you don't try to get it right where it comes out of the pipe."

He soon got the hang of it and was happily lapping away prior to eating his meal. The food was delicious as well, but not because it included slices of fine roast beef or aged porterhouse steaks, neither of which Waggit had ever tasted anyway. It was good because it was the same as the food they used to forage in their park during better times, before they were forced into the Deepwoods End. It seemed that humans threw away similar fare wherever they were, and as he bit into a discarded pretzel covered in mustard, his nose tingled and it brought back happy memories.

When he finished the meal, he licked his lips and paws and let out a sigh of contentment. The haven was safe and comfortable, and his group, the part of the team for whom he was responsible, looked relaxed and happy. Magica was grooming Little Two, which she had done since he and Little One were found abandoned in a box on one cold winter's morning. Little One, the more independent of the two brothers, was listening with fascination to a heated conversation between Cicero and Pilodus. Lowdown was explaining to Gordo how you balanced on a skateboard. He did this with the air of an expert, even though it had been only a couple of hours since he had mastered it himself. From the nervous expression on the big dog's face, Gordo seemed to think it a skill he was unlikely to ever possess. Alona and the receptor were huddled in a corner whispering to each other. Waggit had no idea what they were talking about, and realized he would *never* know what they were talking about. It had already occurred to him that receptors were the closest thing to loners in the world of the Ductors.

He looked at these animals with immense fondness, but he realized that his relationship to them had changed. The sense of responsibility he felt toward them was new and both exciting and scary at the same time. It was something he had never asked for or even dreamed of, and in fact when Tazar had designated him as his successor, he had been the one most surprised of the whole team. He noticed that they had also changed in the way they reacted to him. They now deferred to him more than before, and accepted his decisions without question, except, of course, for Lowdown, who accepted nobody's decisions without question, not even Tazar's. In fact the old dog now played the same role for Waggit as he had for Tazar—that of a wise counselor.

One by one the dogs settled down for the night, which, of course, was actually the day in their new schedule. Waggit missed seeing sunlight, and was looking forward to being in green places under blue skies once more. Nevertheless he slept well until Cicero woke him several hours later.

"Waggit," he said. "Time to move on. Let's get the group together."

Waggit was reluctant to leave this safe place and face the uncertainties of the journey, but he was also looking forward to being reunited with Tazar and the rest of his friends. Cicero had told him that the two parts of the team would come together again at the next haven, which, if all went well, would be the final stop before reaching the new park. So he got up and started to nudge his sleepy companions with his nose. One by one they sprang into wakefulness, and after drinking water and taking care of some casual grooming, they were ready to leave. Little One, who had taken on the role of keeper of the skateboard, grasped it in his mouth and took it back to the flat surface of the blacktopped path. Lowdown followed him, hobbling painfully over the rocks.

The haven had one disadvantage—it was at the end of a dead-end path. While this added to the security of the location, it also meant that the dogs had to retrace their steps in order to get back under the highway that bordered it. But the night was pleasant; the humidity had dropped, and a soft breeze came off the river, ruffling the dogs' coats. With Pilodus in the lead, they came to where the park broadened out. Just before they were about to make a left turn and follow the path under the highway, Waggit stopped dead in his tracks.

"Wait," he said to Pilodus. He turned to Magica. "Do you smell that?" he asked her.

"Can it be?" she said. "Could she really be back?"

"I think I smell her," Alona chimed in.

"Me . . . ," said Little One.

". . . too," added Little Two, although the pair had no idea what the other dogs were talking about.

Cicero joined them from his tail-end position in the group.

"What's going on?" he asked.

"We think we smell a friend," answered Waggit.

Cicero lifted his head, his nose twitching as it picked up the scents that flowed into it.

"The only dogs I smell here are the ones in our group," he said, "especially Gordo."

Had he been able to, Gordo would have blushed at hearing this. He was not known to have the highest standards of personal hygiene.

"No," Waggit assured Cicero, "this isn't a dog; it's an Upright."

Cicero and Pilodus looked at each other in alarm.

"An Upright?" said Pilodus in astonishment. "You're friends with an Upright?"

"If you find that surprising," said Waggit, "wait until you meet her, if it *is* her."

Leaving the two Ductors in a state of confusion, Waggit and Magica cautiously moved forward, following their noses toward the place where the park dropped sharply down to the river. As they came to the verge, they saw it—the familiar tent that had been hidden within the cover of a willow tree in the park the previous summer. It was now pitched on a shallow plateau between the park and the water's edge. Quivering with excitement, Magica was poised to run toward it, but Waggit restrained her with his shoulder.

"Better to be a little cautious," he warned her, and then the two of them moved slowly forward in a low-slung, crouching position, almost as if they were tracking prey. As they got closer, their noses detected the smell they were hoping for, and their ears picked up the memorable sound of soft snoring, almost like a cat's purr. Unable to restrain herself any longer, Magica let out a howl of joy.

"Felicia!" she cried.

11
Danger at Night

A scuffling, grunting noise came from the interior of the tent, followed by a muffled "Magica? Is that you?" Then they heard the sound of zipper being unfastened, and out of one end of the tent a disheveled and sleepy head emerged. It was that of a middle-aged woman whose voice and manner seemed to suggest a privileged background at odds with her tousled appearance. Before she could get any more of her body out of the tent, Magica was all over her, wagging her tail and licking the woman's face, ears, and hair in an expression of pure joy.

"Oh my goodness," spluttered the woman. "It's good to see you too, but let me get out of here so that I can take a look at you."

Waggit seemed thrilled to see the human as well; his whole body rippled with excitement, and the thick, oversize tail for which he was named beat the air frantically.

"Felicia," he cried, "I thought we'd never see you again!"

"And why did you think that?" Felicia asked. "Didn't I tell you when I left last fall that I'd be back in the summer? Didn't you trust me?"

"But with the move and everything, and not being able to leave word for you, I thought you would never find us if— I mean when you returned," he said.

By this time Felicia had emerged like a gigantic stick insect coming out of a cocoon. When she stretched to her full height, she was very tall and skinny, but these were not the things about her you noticed first. She wore an extraordinary combination of clothes, including the largest pair of shorts ever made. They came down well below her knees and went almost up to her armpits, and were held up by two head scarves, one bright red and one citrus green, that functioned as make-do suspenders. The combination of these and the pair of gigantic work boots on her feet made her look like a very underfed clown. She also had on yellow tights with black polka dots, and the whole outfit was topped off with a shawl made of antique lace that looked quite valuable, and as if it had been in her family for a long time. She looked lovingly at the dogs who now surrounded her—all except for Cicero and Pilodus, who stood to one side, confused as to what was happening.

"Well," she said, with a twinkle in her eyes, "you guys don't make it easy for a woman to find you, but I'm glad I did. I think I must have been to every park in Manhattan."

"We're sorry, Felicia," said Magica. "We wouldn't have caused you so much trouble, but we honestly never thought you would come back. You see, we don't have much experience with Uprights keeping their promises."

"Well, I'm one who always will," Felicia assured her.

At this point a low growl came out of Cicero's throat.

"Waggit," he said, "can we have a word?'

Waggit went over to the two puzzled Ductors. He had a smile on his face as he approached them, because he knew exactly what was coming next.

"Waggit," said Cicero, "is it my mistake, or are you carrying on a conversation with that Upright?"

"Oh yes," Waggit replied innocently. "We've known her for some time. She's an old friend."

"Whether you know her or not isn't my point," said Cicero. "My point is that you understand what she says and she understands what you say."

"Oh yes," repeated Waggit. "It's so much easier to have a conversation that way."

"But she's an Upright!" barked Cicero in frustration. "And Uprights don't understand us—it's a well-known fact!"

"Well, this one's different," said Waggit. "You'll never meet another Upright like Felicia, trust me."

"Where did you meet her?" inquired Pilodus.

"It's a long story," Waggit replied. "I'd escaped from a place many realms from here, much farther than we've gone so far. I was alone and trying to get back to the park, when I came across her living in her cloth den. I was as surprised as you are that she knew how to talk to dogs, but she told me that she learned it from a very old Upright—a female—when she was young. We traveled back to the park together. Actually," he admitted, "I don't think I would've made it without her. She stayed with us until the chill and then went somewhere called South, where it's warmer, because she can't stand the long cold."

"But do you trust her?" asked Cicero.

"More than you," said Waggit. "And that doesn't mean I don't trust you either. It just means that she's never let me down, or any of the team."

Cicero and Pilodus looked unconvinced.

"Come on," said Waggit, "let me introduce you."

The Ductors warily followed Waggit to where Felicia was standing.

"I'd like you to meet Cicero and Pilodus," said Waggit. "They're members of the Ductors, and they're the ones who are helping us get to the new park. Without them we wouldn't have got this far."

"Cicero and Pilodus from the Ductors," Felicia

repeated with a smile. "How very Roman. Is your leader named Caesar?"

Felicia often said things that the dogs didn't understand. The Tazarians were so used to it that they ignored her when it happened, but Cicero and Pilodus became even more perplexed.

"No," said Cicero. "He's called Beidel."

"Well, I'm very pleased to meet you," Felicia said warmly. "Thank you for taking care of my good friends." She turned to Waggit and Magica. "Where is the rest of the team, by the way?"

"We had to split up into two groups to make it easier and safer to travel," Waggit explained. "But we'll all be together again at the next haven."

"I can't wait to see everyone else," said Felicia. "That is, of course, if Cicero and Pilodus don't mind me coming along for the ride."

The Ductors were still so bewildered that the only reaction Felicia got was a shrug of Pilodus's shoulders. She took this to mean it was okay. She turned back to the Tazarians.

"I was sorry to hear you had to leave the park," she said. "It must have been awful to give up your realm, but it sounded like life was becoming impossible there."

"How did you hear about it?" asked Magica.

"I came to find you in the Deepwoods," she explained, "and when I saw that the Ruzelas had mended the pipe, I knew that you must've moved; a loner told me that you'd left the park altogether."

"The Ruzelas did what?" asked Waggit.

"They mended the pipe," said Felicia, "the one where you used to live. There was water flowing through it into the pool when I saw it. Wasn't that why you moved?"

"No, it wasn't," said Waggit, "but it would have been a really good reason to."

"Waggit," said Cicero, "we've really got to get moving if we're going to reach the haven before light. If you want this Upright to come with us, she should get her stuff together now."

"Of course," said Felicia. "It'll just take me two minutes."

The dogs had no idea how long two minutes was, but they assumed it wasn't a very long period of time or Felicia wouldn't have mentioned it. She quickly took down the tent, stowed it in its cover, packed her backpack, and was ready to go. They were a strange sight: a tall, skinny, strangely dressed woman accompanied by nine mixed-breed dogs, walking through the streets of New York in the early hours of the morning. The Ductors were wary of Felicia's presence, and they moved nervously along the sidewalk. The dogs still had to observe the caution they had shown before a human was added to the group, and Felicia knew from her own experience that she would be considered a suspicious figure to any passing patrol car, even without the accompanying animals.

"You know," she said after walking next to them for about fifteen minutes, "I'm actually adding to your danger, because there's no way I can make myself inconspicuous like you do. I'll walk on the opposite side of the street, and that way if I attract any attention, it will take it away from you."

This seemed like a sensible idea, and Cicero and Pilodus seemed especially relieved when Felicia crossed to the other side of the road. They were heading north along one of the wide avenues into an area that was more industrial than the residential districts they had passed through before. No sooner were they moving in this new formation than a police car cruised slowly by. The two officers inside peered at Felicia. She walked on, flashing them a warm smile and a slight wave of her hand. The car pulled to a stop and one of the policemen got out. The dogs on the opposite sidewalk froze under parked cars, barely daring to breath.

"Good morning, ma'am," the patrolman said to Felicia. "Do you have any ID on you?"

"I certainly do, officer," said Felicia. "If you'll just hang on a minute."

She rummaged under her clothing and finally revealed a money belt that was hidden beneath several layers. Out of it she took a tattered driver's license and passed it to the cop. He looked at it with a puzzled expression on his face.

"You're a long way from home," he said.

Felicia leaned over and looked at the document as if she wasn't sure why he'd said this.

"Ah, yes," she replied. "Well, you see, I haven't lived at that address for some time."

"What is your present address?" he asked.

"Well, I guess pretty much where I'm standing right now," she decided.

"You mean," said the cop, "that you're homeless, right?"

"Well," Felicia replied thoughtfully, "I suppose in a

technical sense you're right, except that I am without a permanent residence as a matter of choice rather than necessity."

"That may or may not be true," continued the officer, "but the fact of the matter is that you *are* homeless, and there are certain vagrancy laws that apply to folks in your situation in New York City. If you have no visible means of support, I'll have to take you into custody."

"By visible means of support you mean money, credit cards, that sort of thing?"

"That sort of thing, right," agreed the policeman.

Felicia dove back into her money belt and extracted from it a small bundle of dollar bills and a piece of plastic. The cop looked at both in amazement, comparing the name on the credit card with the name on the license and the photo on the license with Felicia herself.

"Is this your credit card?" he asked in amazement.

"Yes," she said, "but I rarely use it. I don't like living with debt."

The officer clearly did not know what to make of her.

"Why are you walking through here at this time

of the morning?" he asked.

"Well, I'm making my way upstate and I wanted to get an early start," she replied, not altogether truthfully.

"Lady, it's three fifteen a.m.!"

"Well, that's early enough, isn't it?" she said innocently.

He gave her back her license, credit card, and money.

"This neighborhood ain't the safest place for a woman to be by herself at this time of night," he said. "If you're going to travel like this, you should probably get yourself a dog or something."

"You know, officer," Felicia said with a smile, "I probably will."

"You do that, and have a nice day." And he got back into the car and drove off.

Felicia sat down on the curb.

"Phew," she said. "That was close. I'm sorry to have exposed you to that kind of risk. Why don't you go on ahead and I'll keep following from the other side of the street, but I'll hang back a bit."

Then Waggit had a good idea, which sounded as if he had understood what the policeman had been saying, though of course he hadn't.

"You know," he said, "an Upright with nine dogs is strange, right? But an Upright with two dogs is nothing special. Why don't two of us travel with you? That'll make you safer, and it'll be two less dogs who have to sneak along, which makes things easier for the others."

"I have an even better idea," said Felicia. "Why don't I put the board in my backpack and carry Lowdown? I can still walk with two others, and then that only leaves six to travel undercover."

The dogs thought this was an excellent plan, especially Lowdown. The novelty of the skateboard had now worn off, and he found it almost as tiring to balance on it as to walk, though not as painful. When the board was safely stowed in her backpack, Felicia attached two pieces of string to Gordo and Alona, the dogs who had volunteered to walk with her. As she explained to them, the last thing she wanted was another run-in with the authorities because of local leash laws. She then scooped up Lowdown and settled him under her arm.

"You're heavier than you look," she commented.

"And smarter," Lowdown retorted. "Just be glad it's me with the tired old legs and not Gordo."

The strange caravan continued its journey. They were in a neighborhood that had once been a bustling industrial and commercial area but was now abandoned and decaying. They passed a former factory building, its long line of windows mostly smashed out and its walls decorated with scrawls of graffiti. Here and there wrecked cars littered the streets, some burned and others vandalized. In some ways the desolation of the area was a benefit to the dogs. There was no one on the street except for the occasional homeless person, who seemed as intent upon remaining unnoticeable as they were. The danger of this bleak environment was that there were no friendly passersby. Anyone the dogs met would likely be up to no good, especially the gangs that often roamed the area, according to Cicero and Pilodus.

But the big advantage of the place was the number of buildings that could be used as havens. Almost any one of the structures they saw would offer shelter to traveling animals, but there was one that the Ductors favored. In its heyday it had been a busy factory, manufacturing screws and bolts, but now it was in the same sad state of decay as its neighbors.

A chain-link fence with two padlocked gates surrounded the whole structure, but there were several places where the fence had been broken open, and the dogs filed one by one into the yard. It was one of those situations where dogs had an advantage over people. There was no break in the enclosure big enough to allow Felicia through.

"I'll just pop 'round the back and see if there's a wall I can climb over or something," she said cheerily, and disappeared around the back of the building after putting Lowdown back on the pavement. Pilodus led the dogs to a side entrance, carefully hugging the wall. The yard was lit with powerful lights that cast a yellowish orange glow, but the interior of the building was as black and dark as anywhere Waggit had ever been. Even though Pilodus had used this haven many times, he was always cautious when approaching it. The receptor had told him that it had been vandalized a number of times. All the copper piping had been stolen, and most of the machinery, and although there was little of value left to take, it was smart to be careful. Everyone was relieved when a black and white dog with a huge mane of hair poked his head out of the doorway and said, "It's okay. Everything's safe."

It was then that they heard Felicia's screams.

12

Reunited

The screams were scary anyway, but because Waggit knew Felicia so well, they were especially frightening. He had watched her in tough situations before, and she had always kept her cool. He had only ever seen her break down once, and that was after they told her about the death of Lug when he was killed in the fight with Tashi. To hear the terror in her shouts now was alarming.

"Quick," he yelled, "follow me! Felicia needs us."

And without thinking about what they might find, the dogs all turned and ran with him back through the hole in the fence through which they had come just moments before. Even Lowdown hobbled after them, not because he could contribute to the group's fighting power, but because there was nobody better at coming up with an instant battle plan.

Once they were on the other side of the fence, the dogs raced around the building. As they turned the far corner, they were faced with a sight that froze the blood in their veins. In front of them were five or six young men and one older one. He was holding Felicia from behind, with one hand over her face, trying to smother her screams, and the other hand pressing the blade of a knife to her throat.

"Stoners!" cried Waggit.

"Be careful," warned Magica. "They've got silver claws."

The dogs barked ferociously at the men and then crouched into attack position, ready to spring.

"Get her money!" yelled the older man to the others. "I know she's got some. It's hidden on her somewhere."

But the younger men had seen the dogs and were backing off.

"Never mind those mutts!" shouted Felicia's attacker.

"They ain't gonna hurt you, but I will if you don't get the money."

"But I'm scared of dogs," whimpered one of the tougher-looking Stoners.

"Oh, poor me, I'm scared of dogs," mocked the older man in a whiny voice. "Well, be more scared of this." He took the knife away from Felicia's throat and pointed it at the frightened young man.

"Go, Waggit," said Lowdown who had been watching the action. "Go now!"

Without another word Waggit leaped toward the man's hand. Before Felicia's attacker could return the knife to her throat, Waggit's jaws trapped his wrist, and he bit down with all his might. The man howled in agony.

"Get him off me," he cried to his sidekicks, who were torn between their fear of the dogs and their even greater fear of the older man. They started kicking at the animals, trying to keep the dogs away as they inched toward their leader. It was at this point that Gordo threw his considerable weight against the back of the man's knees, causing him to come crashing down, bringing Felicia with him. Waggit was still clamped to the man's wrist, while Gordo, not the fastest mover at the best of times, was unable to get away from the two humans before they fell and was now squashed underneath both of them. The other dogs were snarling and snapping at the young men when Alona looked up and cried, "Tazar!"

Sprinting around the building toward the tumult came the rest of the team, led by Tazar. The sight of reinforcements was too much for the young men, who ran for their lives in all directions. The older one released Felicia and tried to scramble to his feet, kicking Waggit in the stomach. This had the effect the man was hoping for. Waggit had to let go of his wrist, and the knife clattered to the ground. Without bothering to pick it up, the would-be mugger ran off, nursing his injured arm.

Despite the retreat of their attackers, there was still chaos at the scene, with Felicia sitting on the ground, Waggit next to her trying to get his breath back, and the other dogs yelping in victory, ecstatic to be reunited with their teammates. Everyone was licking everyone else. Finally Tazar walked up to Felicia, who still hadn't made it to her feet.

"Lady Felicia," he said graciously, "it's good to see you again, even under such troubling circumstances."

"It's always good to see you, Tazar," Felicia replied breathlessly, "but never more so than now."

"Where did you find Waggit and his group?" asked Tazar.

"Actually they found me," she replied. "I was making a tour of every park in the city trying to find you. We met at the one that runs beside the river just a few hours ago, although I must say it seems longer."

"How did you get separated from them?" he asked.

"Looking for a way into the yard," she answered. "As you can see, I don't fit into any of the holes in the fence."

"Ah, it's a pity you didn't go the other way," said Tazar. "There's a gate there that even someone as tall as you can fit through. Follow me."

Felicia staggered to her feet, and with the black dog leading, the entire entourage made its way to the opposite side of the building. Sure enough, halfway along there was a gate that had almost completely fallen off its hinges and now leaned in an open position. They all filed through it and entered the haven.

It took a few moments for their eyes to adjust to the blackness inside the building, but once they became used to the gloom, they could see that they were in a huge open space that once was the heart of the factory. The remains of some wrecked machines lay in parts on the floor, but anything valuable had been stolen long ago. The dogs were so delighted and relieved to be together again that they paid scant attention to their surroundings. Even Gruff, who was the grouchiest dog anyone had ever met, seemed quite pleased to see his teammates, and so were Cicero and Pilodus when they found Dragoman and Naviga.

The receptor, however, was far from happy. He might have had the mane of a lion, but he certainly didn't have the heart of one.

"Oh no, oh no, oh no," he fretted to no one in particular. "Oh my, oh my, I can't stand it when things like that happen. I don't like attracting attention. I know there aren't many people around, but you never know. It's not good to create a stir. It brings down the tone of the location."

Looking around, you would have thought it impossible for this desolate place to become worse, but Waggit had noticed that receptors seemed to be overly sensitive about the spots they were in charge of. As with most havens, this one had good points and bad points, and sometimes they were the same. Here the isolation made it safer because there were fewer human beings, and yet that also made it more dangerous, because those people who were in the area were usually up to no good. The same applied to the food supply: A lack of humans meant a lack of trash for scavenging. Because of this the haven had to have a stash nearby, and the food that it contained had to be brought in from other areas, a time-consuming and dangerous process. But there was always an extra source of sustenance. As they settled in, the dogs heard the telltale rustle of rats.

"Scurries!" said Raz gleefully.

"Fresh meat!" said Cal.

In no time at all a hunting party was organized, and soon they returned with a meal fit for a queen—but not a human queen. When Felicia was offered some, she looked as if she was about to be sick but managed to overcome it by nibbling on a stale bagel that had been retrieved from the stash. Nobody got much sleep that day. There were stories to be told and plans to be made. Everyone wanted to hear about Felicia's adventures in "South." She was a good storyteller, and the dogs rolled around howling with laughter over the outrageous things that had happened to her, or stayed deathly quiet when she described the scary, perilous parts of her journey. Even the Ductors enjoyed the tales, once they got over the shock of being able to understand what she was saying.

Notes were compared between the two groups, each trying to outmatch the other in the degrees of danger and discomfort they claimed they had suffered on the trip. The reality was that for such a difficult undertaking, everything had gone remarkably smoothly, except for the attack on Felicia. Secretly, the Ductors thought the Tazarians had brought the incident upon themselves by being involved with a human in the first place, even one dogs could understand. When they finally ran out of stories and began to drift off to sleep, a visitor woke them; Beidel had arrived.

He entered like an emperor, with the other Ductors fussing around in attendance, and went straight to Tazar. Waggit had noticed that Beidel rarely spoke to anyone else if a leader was present, and this made the younger dog glad, not for the first time, that Tazar was head of the Tazarians. He couldn't imagine that Beidel was ever fun in the way that Tazar could be, and couldn't imagine him playing the kind of practical jokes that Tazar loved.

"I assume your journey was uneventful," Beidel said, leader to leader.

"It was fine," Tazar complimented him. "Very smooth. You have a good organization."

"It has been honed over many risings and through the passage of many dogs," the other replied. "We live to serve our fellow animals."

Even when he was trying to be humble, Beidel sounded boastful.

"I hear," he continued, "that the only incident didn't involve a dog at all, but an Upright some of your team traveled with. Do you think it's wise to associate with the enemy like that?"

"If it was any other Upright, I would emphatically tell you no," replied Tazar, "but this one is well known to our team and has been a true friend. She is always welcome among us. I would introduce you, but I see that she's sleeping, and like most Uprights, she's difficult to wake."

Felicia was stretched out in her sleeping bag at the far end of the building. As if to emphasize Tazar's comments, she let out a huge snort and rolled over, blissfully unaware that she was the topic of conversation.

"Well, that is a pleasure that will have to be delayed,"

said Beidel, his tone of voice implying he thought it unlikely to be a pleasure and one that he would be happy to delay forever.

"This will be your last haven," Beidel continued, changing the subject. "We should be able to guide you to the new park before the next light."

"The assistance you have given us is greatly appreciated by my team," said Tazar. "If there is any way we can repay you, don't hesitate to call on us."

Beidel smiled. "Thank you for the offer, but I can't imagine any circumstances in which we would need your help."

"Well, you never know," replied Tazar, somewhat put out by this dismissal of his gesture.

It was now quite dark, but still too early for the team to move out, because the planned route went through heavily populated streets that would still be lively at this hour. The dogs hated this part of the night. They were impatient to move, especially since this was the last time they would spend on the road before reaching their new home. Beidel and Dragoman decided that instead of breaking the team into two groups, they would do better to keep them together for this final leg of the journey, and not take separate routes to the new park. They would move the team through in batches, three or four at a time. It would take longer, but at least they would be sure to get all the dogs to their destination at the same time.

To pass the time until their departure, the Ductors and Tazarians talked about differences in their lives. Although they had been together for the past two days, the Ductors had been so focused on leading and the Tazarians on following that neither group had really gotten to know the other. The Ductors weren't the most talkative group, even at the best of times, and secretly Waggit was sure this was because they were street dogs. Living the way they do must be very stressful, he thought, always being so close to Uprights, dealing with streets and traffic and all the other things that had made the journey hard for the park dogs. He remembered fondly the times that he and Lowdown had spent almost the whole day just lying in the sunshine on a rock, watching the comings and goings of the park. This kind of contemplation never seemed like a waste of time to Waggit, but he was fairly sure it was something that street dogs didn't have either the time or the inclination for.

The other thing that was foreign to the Ductors

was hunting, even though, like this haven, many of the places they lived in were infested with rats. The Tazarians' hunting tales fascinated them, but not so much that any of them felt tempted to share the Tazarians' meal.

"So you mean you always have to chase them and kill them?" Pilodus asked incredulously, referring to the small animals that were the park dogs' staple diet.

"Well, yes," Waggit replied. "We've found they don't usually come to us on their own."

"And you eat them right away, like you did tonight?" inquired Cicero.

"No," said Waggit. "We always used to take them back to the pipe. We all share food. It doesn't matter whether you hunted it or not, the rule is that you have to share anything that's big enough to divide up."

"Are they still warm when you eat them?" Dragoman chimed in.

"Not usually, but sometimes," said Waggit.

"Oh, how disgusting!" exclaimed Naviga. "How can you do that?"

"Well, at first it's hard," Waggit admitted, "but you get used to it. If you've ever been really hungry, it's amazing what you'll do."

"Don't they all taste the same?" asked Pilodus.

"Oh no," Gordo assured him. "My favorite's hopper, but that scurry we just had was pretty good too. You should try it sometime."

A shudder ran through Pilodus's body.

"No, thank you," he said firmly.

While this conversation was taking place, Tazar formally introduced Felicia to Beidel. The leader of the Ductors remained wary of her but acknowledged that she had remarkable skills, the likes of which he had never known in a human being before. She was assigned the role of lookout and coordinator for the rest of the journey. Her responsibilities were to warn of danger and to keep the team moving and together. She was eager to be a part of the effort and assured them that her height would allow her to give them the earliest possible signal of potential threats. Everyone agreed to the plan, and the receptor was sent into the yard to listen to the sounds coming from the direction in which they were traveling. After what seemed to be an eternity, he returned and said the two words that were their signal to leave.

"Everything's quiet."

Tazar looked at Waggit and grinned. "One more time, my brother."

And with that the dogs moved out.

13

Disaster, Destination, and Dismay

The first part of the night's journey was as uneventful as the Ductors expected it to be, but as the streets became more residential, the dogs' progress became increasingly difficult. Even in the early hours of the morning, the area was livelier than the more sedate neighborhoods adjacent to the park. More people were on the sidewalks, and there was a surprisingly large number of cars on the road. Waggit began to wonder whether the decision to move the team as one group was a wise one. It had been difficult enough to move seven Tazarians and two Ductors over the past two days, but now there were twice that number. Even Beidel had decided to accompany them on this last part of their journey. Felicia certainly helped by shepherding the dogs along, and Waggit watched her with pride as she escorted a small group across the street like a canine school crossing guard.

Fortunately every inch of the curb was lined with parked vehicles, and so concealment, even for this number of animals, was relatively easy. Waggit lay under one car, waiting for his turn to cross a particularly tricky intersection. From his vantage point he could see Felicia holding up her hand to stop the dogs when she saw traffic approaching, or waving them on when all was clear. He realized how fond he was of her, and that every member of the team shared his affection, even Tazar, whose hatred of humans was legendary. Waggit was conflicted about humans. He had certainly suffered because of them. He had been abandoned in the park by one at an early age; he had been captured by park rangers and sent to the pound, where he had seen many dogs taken from their cages, never to return; and he had witnessed immense cruelty when he and Felicia had rescued Lug from men who had been throwing rocks at him.

And yet for every cruel and thoughtless human act that he had suffered or seen, he could recall an equal number of kind and caring ones. Felicia was exceptional in so many ways that he suspected she was part human and part dog, but she wasn't the only one who had shown him compassion. He had been rescued from the pound by a woman who had befriended him in the park; on his long trek with Felicia the previous year he had met a truck driver named Frosty who had given them a lift for many miles; and then there was the car-service driver named Miguel who gave them a lift in another way. He had cheered them up with his good humor and optimism when their spirits were down. But Waggit also knew that on one level Tazar was right. Humans *were* the enemy if you were a free dog. They seemed frightened of animals that they couldn't control, and dogs living on their own were something that they couldn't tolerate. They were a strange and complicated species, Waggit decided, and he thought it best to stick with dogs. At least you knew where you were with them.

These were the thoughts that drifted through his head when an incident unfolded in front of him in what seemed to be slow motion. Felicia was watching over a junction where three roads intersected, two in the usual crisscross pattern of city blocks, and another that cut across both at an angle. It was the same road that they had sprinted along during the rainstorm, only farther uptown. Beidel, who had been traveling with Tazar, was about to cross when Felicia held up her hand in warning. It was clear to Waggit from Beidel's body language that he wasn't going to take orders from a human. He looked up and down the street and then crossed. What he didn't see was a truck with a load of milk as it barreled toward its next delivery along the diagonal road. Tazar did see it, however, and he raced across the intersection hitting Beidel at full tilt, bowling him over and out of harm's way. The truck swerved and continued on its course, but not before Waggit heard a sickening thump that made his heart stop beating for a second.

Felicia ran into the middle of the road, motioning to the dogs gathered on each side to stay where they were. Waggit came out from under the car and saw Tazar lying on the blacktop. Felicia bent over him, and then very gently she gathered him into her arms and carried him to a bus shelter that was a short distance down the block. Tazar was a large, heavy dog, but Felicia was much stronger than she appeared, and with very little difficulty she laid him down. The dogs, abandoning all caution, gathered around.

"Tazar, Tazar," Felicia said, quietly but urgently. "Can you say something?"

There was no response from the motionless animal. She stroked his head gently and repeated what she had just said. There was still no response, but then, after a couple of minutes that seemed like an eternity, his eyelids fluttered and his big brown eyes looked up at her.

"Is Beidel okay?" were the first words out of his mouth.

Beidel, who was standing nearby, moved forward so that Tazar could see him.

"Thanks to you, Tazar, I'm fine."

"Good," said Tazar. "Because I wouldn't want us both to die. Teams need their leaders."

"Indeed they do," agreed Felicia, "and that's precisely

why you're not going to die."

"Is Waggit there?" Tazar asked, ignoring her last remark.

Waggit pushed forward between the other dogs, his whole body shaking with fear.

"I'm here, Tazar."

"Waggit, I'm done for," the black dog said. "I want you to take over the team. I always intended that you would eventually; I just didn't want it to be this soon. I hope the new park works out for all of you. I would have liked to have seen it."

"Oh, Tazar," said Felicia, "stop being so melodramatic. You got bumped by a truck is all. You'll be fine."

Waggit knew that Tazar could, and often did, exaggerate a situation, but that he was relentlessly stoic about any injury. In his eyes a leader must never show weakness or vulnerability. If Tazar said he was dying, he must have good reason to think so.

"Felicia," Tazar said in a quiet voice, "I can't feel my back legs."

A gasp went through the dogs, and nobody said a word.

"Well, in that case we have to get you some help,"

Felicia said after a moment's thought. "Waggit, go with the Ductors and settle the team in the new park. I'm pretty sure I know where it is from listening to their description. I'm going to take Tazar to some Uprights who can make him better."

"I don't want to go near any Uprights, Felicia," growled Tazar. "I'd sooner die here with honor."

"Oh, don't be silly," Felicia replied irritably. "They're not going to do anything to you that will harm you—I'll make sure of that. And then when you're better, we'll get you back with the team and everything will return to normal. Besides," she added, "I don't see what's so honorable about dying here in a bus shelter."

"She's right, boss," chimed in Lowdown. "If she can get some of her kind to put you back together again, why not do it? She ain't gonna let them take you to the Great Unknown or anything like that. You know you can trust her. Besides, we need you. I mean, Waggit's a fine fellow and all that, but he ain't you—not yet he ain't."

"He's right," said Waggit. "I'm not."

Then Beidel walked over to Tazar and looked into his eyes with great sympathy and respect.

"Tazar," he began, "because of my stupid pride you saved my life, and I will never forget that. As long as I live, the Ductors will protect your team, wherever they are. You have my solemn word on that. You are a fine leader, and leaders like us are rare. We have something that other dogs don't. It can't be acquired; it can only be strengthened over time. Your boy here"——he nodded toward Waggit——"probably has it, but he needs your example and teaching to help him achieve his potential. Don't let him down; don't let your team down; most of all, don't let yourself down. Go with this Upright and let her help you. Your team will be in good paws, I promise you."

After that speech there was nothing left to say. The biggest hurdle now was getting Tazar to the people who could give him the medical attention he needed. It was one thing for Felicia to pick him up and carry him to the bus shelter, but he was far too heavy for her to carry him a long distance. She had no idea where she would find a veterinarian, but in all likelihood it was many blocks from where they were now. Once again, the skateboard came to the rescue. With its broken end it was barely big enough to carry the big black dog, but if he lay on it with his legs sticking out sideways, he could just stay on. Felicia removed one of the scarves that held up her baggy shorts and tied it around the front wheels of the board, declaring as she did that if the worst thing that happened was her pants falling down, then they would be in good shape. Of course this meant that Lowdown would have to make the rest of the journey on his own, but he assured Tazar that he was up to it, and the Ductors said that they weren't too far from the new park anyway.

The last they saw of Felicia and Tazar that day was the strange sight of her dragging their injured chief toward what they all hoped would be his full recovery. Waggit stood next to Beidel as they watched them disappear around a corner.

"He's a fine dog," muttered Beidel.

Waggit realized that this was the first time the other animal had spoken to him directly since their initial meeting. Unless he was giving orders, Beidel only ever conversed leader to leader. This meant one thing: He recognized that Waggit was now in charge of the Tazarians. From this moment on, and until Tazar's return, they were his responsibility.

The accident had cost the group precious time, and Dragoman was eager to get them back on their journey. But Lowdown was still having trouble moving quickly. Even though he gritted his teeth and fought back the pain, his legs were just too stiff to move as fast as the Ductors wanted. The other dogs helped him as best they could; Magica even took his tail in her mouth, lifting his back legs off the ground and pushing him forward like a rather scruffy wheelbarrow. But however they tried to ease him along, it was still slow going, and their guides kept looking nervously at the night sky for any sign of light.

Finally they came to a curving sidewalk bordered by a high gray stone wall, over which branches hung. Pilodus, who was in the lead, began to run with excitement and didn't stop until he reached a gap in the wall. As the other dogs caught up with him, they saw that this opened onto a path that went up the side of a wooded hill.

"We're here!" Pilodus barked.

The team ran up the hill, yipping with joy. They abandoned the footpath for the pleasure of feeling the earth, leaves, and tree roots beneath their paws, and the smell of green things growing. Even Lowdown was caught up in the excitement and did his best to keep up. The hill ran steeply up to its brow, and it was with high expectations that they ran toward it, impatient to see the view that would unfold before them when they reached the crest. Alicia was the fastest dog on the team by far, but she was also the laziest, and so it was Waggit and Magica who were the first to get there. What they saw made their hearts sink.

Instead of the vastness of the park they were used to, this one occupied a narrow strip of land between the road they had been on and the highway that flanked the wide expanse of the river. Not only was the park small, but most of it was also taken up with formal gardens that surrounded a large building of yellow stone with a tower at one end. Directly in front of them was a blacktop parking lot, sectioned off into large spaces. On the sidewalk in front of these were signs showing that the parking areas were for buses only. The dogs couldn't read the signs, but they recognized the drawings on them. They knew what buses looked like, and they also knew that they were usually filled with people. It seemed this was one of the most people-intensive areas they had ever seen, and as such completely unsuitable for their needs. Alicia said what everyone was thinking.

"Well, wouldja look at that. The gateway to the Great Unknown!"

14

Advice from a Stranger

The dogs wandered unhappily around the parking lot, sniffing halfheartedly at spots where the buses had leaked oil. The area was empty now, but the dogs knew that when daylight came, it would fill with vehicles containing people. They also knew that the same people would immediately call the authorities when they saw a pack of dogs.

"We came all this way for this?" Alicia continued. "Tazar may die for this? What were those dogs thinking?"

"They wasn't thinking," grumbled Gruff. "That's the trouble with dogs nowadays—they never think. It's always act first, think later—if ever."

"What'll we do, Waggit?" asked Cal.

"We can't stay here," added Raz.

"D'you think it's a trap?" Alona wondered.

"We'll fight 'em off . . . ," Little One said.

" . . . if it is," added Little Two.

Waggit knew they were all turning to him as their leader for reassurance and direction. The Tazarians had raced up the hill in their excitement, way ahead of the Ductors, who were just joining them now. Waggit turned to them to get answers to the team's questions, but before he could say a word, Dragoman walked up to him.

"You can't hang around here. We have to move on before the light," he insisted.

"But I thought here was here," said Waggit. "I mean, I thought this was here. What I mean to say is, I thought this was the new park."

"No," said Dragoman, amazed that Waggit would even think it. "You can't live here—it's far too small. No, the park you're going to is next to this. Come on, let me show you."

He walked to the other side of the yellow stone building, with Waggit and the rest of the team following. Lowdown, who had finally caught up, panted and wheezed alongside them. Dragoman stopped on a terrace that was attached to one end of the building. The view, even in the blackness of night, was magnificent, with the broad, stately river dominating the landscape as it wound its way to the sea. This was the highest point of the park, and beneath them the dogs could see the paths that ran down to the surrounding streets. They were outlined in lights that cast an eerie yellowish green glow. The paths ended at a bridge that ran over a road connecting to the highway. On the far side of the bridge was a hill, a huge, black mass of land, without a single light on it to break up its impenetrable darkness.

"That," said Dragoman, pointing his nose toward the hill, "is your new home. That is where you will live."

The Tazarians looked at the hill with a combination of excitement and awe at its vastness. Each of them was lost in his or her own thoughts until Lowdown broke the silence.

"I hope there's some flat bits," he said, "because I

ain't got the legs what can go up and down that all day."

The dogs' laughter cut through their apprehension, and they began to make their way down to the bridge. When they got to it, the Ductors stopped. Beidel turned toward Waggit.

"We will go no farther," he said. "I made a promise to Tazar back there that I will keep. If you need help, send one of your dogs to this place, but only during the time of darkness. This is not our realm, but we have good relations with the Terminors, and the streets around the park are in their realm. They have dogs who patrol here each darkness, and they will get the message back to me." He looked up at the looming mass of the hill and shuddered. "Good luck here," he continued. "I hope it meets your needs, though it's not a place I'd choose."

Then he stretched forward on his two front legs and bowed down in a gesture of farewell, and with that the Ductors turned and made their way back up the path toward the yellow stone building. They had gone only a few feet when Waggit called out to them.

"Beidel," he cried, "thank you. Thank you to all

the Ductors for bringing us here. We're in your debt forever."

"No," answered Beidel. "Tazar canceled any debt back there. You owe us nothing."

The Ductors continued up the path, watched by the Tazarians until they disappeared over the top of the hill and were gone. Waggit turned to the team.

"Let's find out what our new home is like," he said, trying to sound as excited and optimistic as possible.

They trooped over the bridge and entered a thick wood with only narrow paths. Even though the sky was beginning to lighten, beneath the canopy of leaves above their heads it was still as black as Tazar's coat. But the most noticeable thing about the new environment was the smell. To dogs, with their extraordinary noses, the way something smells is more important than the way it looks, and this place smelled wilder than anywhere else in the city that they'd ever been. They could smell and hear the presence of many animals of all sizes, and that promised good hunting; they could also smell the pungent odor of dead leaves that had lain where they were for years, undisturbed by leaf blowers, rakes, or any of the other tools park workers used to clean and tidy. The dogs could only faintly smell the scent of humans. Some had passed through the woods, but not enough to leave the over-powering smell that had filled the air in their former home, even in the Deepwoods End. So far, this new park felt good.

Waggit led the team along the narrow path, look-ing for a clearing where they could rest. He knew that his dogs were getting tired, drained of energy by both the stress of the journey and the shock of Tazar's acci-dent. The trail ascended sharply, and the incline made it slow going for tired legs. He decided they couldn't go any farther and divided the team in two, putting one half on either side of the pathway, hidden by the ferns that grew beneath the trees. He placed Cal and Raz on Eyes and Ears duty and then settled down to sleep himself. He was exhausted but couldn't sleep; he was too wired by the night's events and his new responsibilities. He also longed to be living during the day again. He didn't like this nocturnal existence. He was an animal who needed light, and so he decided to scout out their new home.

The path they had been on continued to wind steeply upward and Waggit decided to follow it. As he climbed, he noticed that there was none of the evidence of humans that was everywhere in their previous park—no archways or benches, no paved footpaths or ball fields. This was raw woodland that had gone almost unchanged for as long as the hill had been there. It was perfect for the dogs with one exception: There was no open space that he could see, no place to run or just lie in the sun. It was late morning, but the only light was filtered through the ceiling of leaves that arched over everything.

Then he felt some deep instinct kick in. It was a tingling in the nose and an itching of the coat that said to him, "This way. Follow me." He cut across the woods away from the path. The going was hard. The same kinds of ferns that were protecting his sleeping team kept getting caught around his legs, slowing him down. Then he came upon a huge cliff made of rock, similar to those they had lived by in Central Park but much bigger and steeper. Waggit was eager to see what was at the top, and he began to scramble up the sharp incline, holding on to tree branches with his teeth to balance himself when he lost his footing.

It was a tough climb and one that could only have been done by a dog as young, strong, and fit as he was. The last few feet were the hardest, when every muscle in his weary body cried out for rest, but with one last massive effort he pulled himself over the rock's edge. What he saw made him gasp. In front of him was dog paradise. The cliff formed the outer perimeter of an open plateau with a magnificent view of the river and the land that extended for many miles from its far bank. A broad meadow thick with sweet-smelling grasses spread out from the rim of the plateau and stretched back to another rock formation on its far end. From this a crystal spring flowed, pouring water that ran into a pool and then tumbled down the hillside in a gurgling stream. Cut into the rocks near the spring were natural caves, and woods surrounded either side of the meadow.

Waggit was elated. This was better than he could ever have imagined, and eagerly he ran across the grass to explore the dark, cavernous holes in the rock. There were four of them that ran in a row at the foot of the outcrop where it met the meadow. The first one he entered was shallow, but with a dry, sandy floor that looked like it was protected from the elements. He moved to the next one, peering into its dim interior. It was only a little bigger than the first, but the one next to it appeared to open up into a much larger space.

Cautiously, he entered. Once through the narrow entrance it became a cave so big that until his eyes became accustomed to the gloom, he could not make out its roof or walls. As he moved forward, the scratching of his claws on the sandy floor echoed loudly, however softly he walked. Suddenly he stopped. Staring at him from deep within the cave was a pair of yellow eyes that followed his every movement. He couldn't make out the rest of the animal, so he stepped to one side, allowing light to flood into the cavern. He drew in his breath as a wave of fear ran through his body. There in front of him, lying still and impassive, was the silhouette of a huge and magnificent timber wolf. Waggit averted his eyes from the wolf's stare in a gesture of submission.

"I am Waggit," he said, still not daring to lift his head.

"I know," replied the wolf in a resonant voice.

"How?" asked Waggit. "How do you know?"

"I am a Gray One," replied the wolf. "This and many other things I know."

For as long as he had been with the team, Waggit had heard stories of the Gray Ones, mythical creatures of amazing powers who were on this earth to protect the lives of ordinary dogs. No one he knew had ever seen one, and he had assumed that they only existed in the stories handed down from one generation of dogs to the next; yet here he was in the presence of one. Or was he? Waggit dared to glance up briefly. The end of the cave where the wolf was lying was so dark that he could barely make out his shape. Only the intensity of those yellow eyes stopped him from going closer.

"Do you live in this cave?" he asked the wolf.

"I live nowhere and everywhere" came the puzzling reply.

"My team needs a home," Waggit said. "I came here to look for one."

"You have found one," the wolf assured him. "This is your home."

"Here—in this cave?" asked Waggit.

"Does it not feel like your home?" the wolf answered.

Waggit considered the question before saying anything. He examined how he felt in this cool, dark place, and he realized that despite the formidable presence of this powerful creature he felt at peace.

"It does, Gray One," he finally replied. "We could live here in harmony."

"Well, most of you," said the wolf. "I'm not sure Alicia and Gruff will ever find serenity—or even seek it."

Waggit looked up, astonished, all fear of the creature gone. Did he detect a twinkle in those blazing yellow eyes? Did Gray Ones make jokes? He had never heard of such a thing. And how did he know the names of the Tazarians? Then a thought occurred to him.

"You say you know many things, Gray One," he said respectfully. "Tell me this—do you know if Tazar will recover?"

"I know many things, but not everything" came the reply. "Tazar's fate is written for him, as is yours, and he will follow his script as you will follow yours. But now you must sleep. You cannot lead without it. You are a good dog, Waggit, and you deserve your rest."

Waggit suddenly felt more tired than he had ever felt in his life. He lay down without even turning around four times as he usually did, and instantly fell into a deep, dark sleep.

15
Home at Last

Waggit awoke with a start. He had no idea how long he had been sleeping, but the day seemed to be drawing to a close. He sprang to his feet in confusion. His strange dream about the Gray One filled his brain. Or was it a dream? It had seemed so real. He walked to the far end of the cave, but there was no evidence of any such creature having been there. The sun was now lower in the sky, and its rays came horizontally through the entrance, flooding the cave with light. He looked but could see no paw prints, no silver hairs caught against the roughness of the rock, no indication that a wolf had lain in this spot earlier in the day—except for a faint smell, ancient and primal, that lingered in the air and then vanished.

He shook himself fully awake and went out into the meadow. Looking around, he saw a pathway to his left, actually no more than a trail that seemed to wind its way down the hill. He followed it, jumping over fallen trees and at times scrambling down rocky outcroppings. After running for some time, he came upon the path he had taken earlier in the day, the path that had led to the cliff. Retracing his steps, he found a very worried team.

"Oh my dear," cried Magica, "where have you been? We looked all over for you, but not knowing this realm, we didn't know which direction to go in."

"Yeah," screeched Alicia, "and we ain't got no water here, and I'm parched."

"Don't worry yourself, my lady," said Waggit, sounding remarkably like Tazar. "I have found the perfect home for us, a home so good I can scarcely believe it's real."

The dogs crowded around and bombarded him with questions: "How far is it?" "What's it look like?"

"Is there shelter?" "Does another team claim it as their realm?" This last question he couldn't answer, for he didn't know, but he had a feeling that it belonged to them and that they would be unchallenged. As far as he could remember, the Gray One had told him as much. Instead of answering the dogs' questions, he simply said, "Follow me and all will be revealed."

Eagerly they trooped up the path, chattering with excitement. Up and up they went, farther than Waggit remembered, but he assumed that this was because they were moving more slowly than he had on account of Lowdown.

But after a while he began to get worried. All the woods looked the same, and without the well-defined pathways they were used to, it was difficult to tell exactly where they were. He realized that he had missed the trail, and now it was beginning to get dark.

"Stop," he said. "We've got to go back. I made a mistake."

There was a moment of silence, and then some low grumbling.

"Oh no, I'm tired."

"You're tired! I'm tired and hungry."

"And thirsty!"

"Are you sure you didn't dream this place?"

"This ain't as nice as the old park. It's spooky."

Waggit was beginning to realize how hard it was to be a leader, and how easy Tazar made it look most of the time. He wondered if it had been a mistake to admit he'd made a mistake. Whether it was or not, now was the time to be firm.

"We just missed it is all," he said with a confidence that he didn't necessarily feel. "We'll find it if we go back."

And so everyone turned around and went back down the path. They were nervous and jumpy, and the woods were getting darker by the minute. Several times Waggit thought he recognized the way and then realized that he was mistaken. His heart began to pound with fear and anxiety, and the weight of his responsibility became almost unbearable.

Then he saw it. Deep in the woods there was a flash of silver and a blaze of yellow eyes!

"This is it," he cried. "This is the way. We'll soon be there."

And indeed they were. As the trail broke free of the woods and they entered the meadow, a bright full moon appeared, flooding the landscape with its cool, blue light. It made the area look magical, and the dogs stood in stunned silence, which was broken by Magica.

"It's beautiful, Waggit. It's the most beautiful place I've ever seen."

As if released from a spell, the dogs ran around the meadow howling with delight. They ran in and out of the caves and splashed in the pool. Lowdown hobbled up to Waggit and lay down next to him.

"You done good," he said. "It ain't ever gonna get better than this."

"I didn't do anything," Waggit replied. "I mean, anyone could've found this place. I just happened to be the one."

"It ain't just that, although that's major," insisted Lowdown. "It was you who persuaded Tazar to leave in the first place. He'd've never done it without you pushing him. That's one of the good things about being young—you believe you can do anything. By the time you get to my age, you know that you can't, and more and more things seem impossible."

"Lowdown," Waggit said after a pause, "do you believe in the Gray Ones?"

"Certainly," answered Lowdown. "Why wouldn't you?"

"But have you ever seen one?" asked Waggit.

"Just because you've never seen something don't mean it don't exist," replied Lowdown.

"No," said Waggit. "I suppose you're right."

"Not only right, but hungry," said Lowdown. "Time to get a hunting party organized."

The team hadn't eaten anything all day, and it didn't take much to persuade the best hunters to swoop into the woods in search of prey. Even though he was the best of them all, Waggit didn't join the chase. He chose to stay behind with Gordo to scout out suitable locations for Eyes and Ears duty, while Magica and Alona organized the living arrangements. As usual, Gruff's and Alicia's only contributions were to criticize what everyone else was doing, while Lowdown snoozed contentedly. Much as they searched, neither Waggit nor Gordo could find any ideal lookout positions. The rock face surrounding the caves was too high and too sheer to be of any use, and the woods were too far away. Waggit decided that the best thing to do would be to have a sentry posted at the mouth of the large cave.

He had barely reached this conclusion when the hunting party returned. The hunters were ecstatic with what they had found.

"It wasn't like hunting," Raz panted excitedly. "It was more like choosing."

"I never saw so many animals," Cal agreed. "You almost tripped over them."

"Even Little Two got a hopper," said Little One.

"And it was bigger than your nibbler," retorted Little Two.

"If the woods are always this full," said Cal, "I'm not even going to bother with nibblers anymore. They're too small and too full of bones."

The rest of the team agreed that mice weren't worth the effort, even though a few days ago they would have given anything for one. After the meal was consumed and cleared away, the team settled down for what remained of the night. Because they were so far away from any humans, there was no supply of the newspaper and cardboard that usually made up their bedding. Instead, Magica and Alona had pulled up ferns and carefully spread them around the interior of the cave. They wouldn't last as long as paper and cardboard, but they smelled sweeter and were easily replenished from the ones that grew nearby.

Waggit decided that he would take the first watch of Eyes and Ears, and then Gordo would replace him when he got sleepy. He lay down in the entrance to the cave and looked out over the meadow still bathed in moonlight. He felt at peace with the world. The water from the spring chimed musically as it splashed over the rocks; he could hear the deep, slow breathing and the occasional grunt, snore, and even belch of the team sleeping behind him; a soft mild breeze carried the scents of meadow grass and wild honeysuckle into his nostrils. All was well, except that the true leader of the team was not with them. Much as he was enjoying his new responsibilities, Waggit missed Tazar and longed for his return.

Suddenly he heard rustling coming from the woodland to his right. The hackles on his back stiffened with apprehension. Could this be a rival team come to reclaim their territory? He knew it couldn't be Ruzelas, because they would be making far more noise. As he watched, a doe glided slowly and gracefully out into the open meadow, followed by her fawn, still wobbling precariously on young legs. They both set about grazing. Waggit was amazed. He had never seen animals that big in a city park; in fact he had only ever seen deer on his journey back from the country, and had found them a little scary. He growled softly, trying to not wake any of the team. The mother slowly turned her head, gave him a look of indifference, and then continued eating. This was clearly a very different park from the one they were used to.

Shortly before daybreak Waggit felt his eyelids getting heavy, and an overwhelming desire to sleep overtook him once more. He got up and moved as quietly as he could toward Gordo's large slumbering body and nudged him with his nose.

"Whaa . . . ?" mumbled the sleeping dog. "Whassup? Is it breakfast?"

"No," whispered Waggit, "it's time for Eyes and Ears."

"Oh, okay," Gordo said good-naturedly, and lumbered off to the mouth of the cave.

Waggit was just about to settle down to sleep when there was a yell from the new sentry.

"Waggit!" he shouted. "Longlegs. There's Longlegs in the grass."

His cries awakened all the dogs, who ran to the entrance to see what the problem was. Gordo pointed toward the deer with his nose.

"Longlegs," he repeated, "and where there's Longlegs, there's sure to be Uprights."

"That would be true," said Waggit, "if they were Longlegs, but they're not. I can't remember what Felicia called them, but they're not Longlegs, and Uprights don't sit on them, so let's all go back to sleep."

"Sorry, Waggit," said Gordo somewhat shame-facedly. "I just ain't ever seen nothin' like that before."

The deer, while perfectly unconcerned about one dog growling at her, decided that a whole pack was another thing altogether, so she and the fawn skipped hurriedly into the woods. With Gruff complaining about the frequency of false alarms, the dogs returned to their places and tried to get back to sleep before the dawn broke and awoke them all once more.

16
The Curse of Damnation Hill

The next few days the team spent getting to know their new surroundings. Although not as big as the previous park, because of its steepness it was more difficult to get around, which was one of the reasons it wasn't swarming with people. It was particularly hard for Lowdown, who spent most of his days around the cave or in the meadow, rarely venturing farther away. He seemed quite content to pass the time like this, though.

Although it was extremely rare to see humans where

the team lived, it did happen occasionally, and as a result they had to be on their guard at all times. The ones who did venture up their way were usually hardy souls wearing heavy hiking boots and backpacks, often with binoculars around their necks. These were the easiest to avoid, because they spent most of their time staring up in the trees trying to get a glimpse of some birds in the branches.

"I don't know why they spend so much time looking at flutters," Gordo was heard to say one time. "It's not like they eat them or anything."

There were sections of the park that were as full of people as any part of the Skyline End. At its farthest point the park became a long promontory bordered by two rivers, the Wide Flowing Water on one side and a smaller one on the other. Where the hill flattened out as it came to the edge of the water, there were ballparks, playgrounds, gardens, a couple of small snack bars, and all the other aspects of human presence that the dogs tried to avoid. However, it was in areas such as these that dogs could scavenge, and although the Tazarians loved having a ready supply of fresh meat, sometimes they just longed for pizza.

On one such scavenging expedition they came into contact with the Terminors for the first time. Gordo, Cal, Raz, and Waggit were searching for tasty human food in the trash cans near one of the ballparks. Their noses had indicated that one possibly contained delicious morsels, and even though Gordo had used his considerable weight against it, he was unable to knock the container over because, like many of the others, it was chained to a bench. They were discussing other possible methods of liberating the food when they heard a low growl behind them.

"Hey, you guys," said the owner of the growl, "I hope you know this is our realm."

They turned to see a small but fearless-looking dog fiercely staring them in the eyes. He was part Chihuahua, part who-knows-what, and one of those little dogs who use aggression to make up for their lack of size. Waggit stared him down.

"And which realm would that be?" he asked.

"The realm of the Terminors, thank you for asking," replied the dog with a sneer, "and thank you for leaving."

"I thought," said Waggit, "that the Terminors were

street dogs, not park dogs."

"We are," agreed the other, "and over there is one of our streets."

He nodded toward a road that led into this part of the park.

"But this," said Raz, joining the conversation, "is part of the park."

"I ain't gonna argue with you, brother," growled the little dog. "I'm telling you—this is our realm and you're not welcome here."

"Welcome or not," said Gordo, stretching himself up to his full height, "we *are* here, and if you give us any more trouble, I'll sit on you."

Even this dire threat didn't seem to faze the little guy.

"Listen, fatty, you don't scare me. You move one paw print closer and I'll get the rest of my team, and then let's see you throw your weight around."

"Slow down a moment," Waggit cut in. "We were told by Beidel that if we needed help, we should get in touch with your team—you would be there for us. You don't seem especially helpful at the moment."

"Beidel?" questioned the Terminor, looking nervous for the first time. "You know Beidel?"

"Sure we do," said Cal. "The Ductors brought us here."

"Wait a moment," said the Terminor. "Are you those crazy dogs living on the hill?"

"We are dogs," Waggit assured him, "and we do live on the hill, but I don't think we're any more crazy than any other dogs."

"If you live on that hill you are," said the Terminor. "Either that or ignorant."

"Ignorant of what?" asked Waggit.

"The Curse," replied the Terminor, "the Curse of Damnation Hill—your new home. They didn't tell you about that before bringing you here?"

"No," said Waggit. "That seems to be something they forgot to mention. Tell us about it."

"Well, it ain't a pretty story, let me say that," said the dog. "My name's Cabrol, by the way, and I apologize for being a little harsh just then."

Waggit introduced himself and the other Tazarians, and then Cabrol continued with the tale.

"This all happened many risings ago, before any of us were born, or even those who went before us. The way I heard it is that an old, old Upright used to live on the hill. He had long whiskers, and ate only berries

and tree roots and stuff like that and never went anywhere. Then one day a team of Wild Yellows came to
the hill."

"Wild Yellows!" exclaimed Waggit, who had never
heard of coyotes being in the city. "How did they get
here?"

"Who knows," said Cabrol. "Like I said, this was
many risings ago, maybe even before the Uprights built
their dens around here. Perhaps they swam over from
the Far Distant Territories; with Wild Yellows you
never know, but for sure they was here. Anyway, they
came across the ancient Upright, and they scared him,
and he started to throw rocks and stuff at them. So
they attacked, which of course you would if someone's
throwing things at you. But being Wild Yellows, they
got to howlin' and nipping and torturing the old one.
There's something comes over them that they can't
control—it's like a blood lust, and once that's up, they
don't know how to stop it. So they killed him, and
he died a hard death. But just before he passed on, he
cursed them and their species forever. Now, whether
you like it or not, we are the same kind, and the Curse
lives on to this day."

The Tazarians were silent as they tried to take in

this alarming information.

"What happened to the Wild Yellows?" Waggit finally asked.

"Nobody knows," replied Cabrol. "But what we do know is that any dog who's tried to live there since then—well, let's just say strange things have happened to them."

"Strange things like what?" asked Cal nervously.

"They got sick," said Cabrol, "or trees fell on them or rocks came crashing down the cliff and hit them. Some just disappeared and were never seen again. No dogs have ever lived there longer than one Change. If they came during the Chill, they left before the Long Cold."

"Waggit, this is terrible," cried Gordo.

"It's only terrible if it's true," Waggit reassured him.

"Hey," Cabrol said, "I wouldn't lie to you. Why would I do that?"

"I'm not saying you're lying," replied Waggit. "All I'm saying is that when stories get told, sometimes they get changed in the telling, and what you end up with isn't exactly the same as what happened."

"These wasn't all stories, Waggit," said Cabrol solemnly. "I knew some of them personally."

There was really nothing they could think of to say after that, and so the Tazarians left Cabrol and started back up the path toward the hill they now knew was called Damnation Hill. They were so disturbed by what the Terminor had said that they even forgot to get the food out of the trash can. By now it was quite dark, and as they struggled up the narrow track that led to the meadow, Waggit stopped and turned to the other three.

"What we heard just now," he warned, "I don't think we should tell the rest of the team. For one thing, it may not be true, and for another, if it is true, there's nothing we can do about it right now."

The other dogs all agreed this was the sensible thing to do, even though Waggit knew there was little chance that Cal or Raz would keep the information to themselves and practically no possibility that Gordo would.

Their worries about the stories Cabrol told soon took second place to an event that was far more important than the legend of the hill, something that eclipsed all others. Like many of life's important occasions, it happened on a very ordinary day. Cal, Raz, Little One, and Little Two had all volunteered to go out hunting, which usually meant they would chase a few squirrels for the fun of it and come back saying they hadn't seen anything worth going after. Magica had decided to clean out the cave. She had removed all the old ferns, most of which had gone brown with age while Alona pulled up new ones to replace them. Gordo, who was at his happiest when he was doing something for Magica, was sweeping out the areas she had cleaned up. Holding a branch with a few leaves on one end in his mouth, he moved his head from side to side so that the leaves could brush the sandy floor of the cave. Whether or not this made their home cleaner was hard to say. What was certain was that it irritated both Gruff and Alicia. Gruff had been struck several times by Gordo with his enthusiastic but poorly aimed whisks of the branch, and Alicia was in the middle of a sneezing fit brought on by the clouds of dust that Gordo's "broom" created.

Lowdown and Waggit were lying in the sun idly talking about this and that when Waggit suddenly pricked his ears and stood up. The first thing he saw was the top of the broken skateboard, and then, as she slowly climbed up the steep track that led to the meadow, more and more of Felicia was revealed. The skateboard was jammed into her backpack, and she was wearing a new hat with a wide brim and a fold of material that hung down the back, covering her neck. Her face was red with exertion and she was puffing loudly, but she had a broad smile on her face.

"You couldn't find anywhere more difficult to locate or to get to?" she asked, climbing up the last few feet.

She sat down on a fallen tree trunk at the edge of the meadow, wiping the sweat off her forehead with a large green handkerchief. As she did, the dogs ran over to her yelping with joy, even Gruff and Alicia. The commotion they made filled the woods, and their sounds were carried to where the so-called hunters were playing. Soon they joined the crowd of dogs, so that the entire team was milling around Felicia. They peppered her with questions that came so fast, she could barely answer one before she got hit with another.

"Where have you been?"

"What have you been doing?"

"How did you find us?"

"Where's Tazar?"

It was Waggit who asked the last question, and the team went silent, because they knew that the answer would be crucial to all of them. Felicia answered it by rising to her full height and looking back down the trail that she had been on.

"Unless I'm very much mistaken," she said, "there's a dog coming up this way who looks remarkably like him. Excuse me," she called down the trail, "but are you Tazar?"

"Always have been, my lady," came a familiar voice, "and with a bit of luck I hope I always will be."

17

Restored

Not only was the team pleased to see Tazar, but also they were relieved. While there wasn't a dog among them who would have told you that Waggit had been anything less than an exemplary leader in the black dog's absence, nevertheless something had been missing, and they were overjoyed to be reunited with Tazar. Dogs like things to stay the same, to have a structure that they recognize, and however good a substitute Waggit had been, he was still just that— a replacement leader, not *the* leader. Waggit himself would have been the first to agree with this.

But when they saw Tazar coming up the steep track, they realized that even with his return things would never be quite the same. The once-agile dog now limped on one back leg, and moved slowly and with difficulty. Waggit suspected that the skateboard had done as much service for Tazar as it ever had for Lowdown. But even though the shock of his disability sent a collective shudder through the team, the delight they all felt at his survival soon overcame it. Now it was Tazar's turn to be peppered with questions. He clearly enjoyed being the center of attention once again. But as he told his story, he needed considerable help from Felicia to fill in the blanks.

"After the big roller hit me, Felicia took me to this . . . what was the place called?"

"Veterinary hospital," said Felicia.

"Whatever." Tazar shrugged. "Anyway, this place where they fix up dogs who are sick or hit by rollers like I was. So I'm lying on this platform and an Upright comes over to me, and he's an Upright and I'm a free dog, so I growl at him—I mean, any dog would, wouldn't he?"

There was a general murmur of agreement that this

was the appropriate way to deal with an approaching Upright.

"As it turns out, he doesn't want to fight, but instead he jabs me with this sharp thing and suddenly I don't want to fight him either, because I feel pretty good."

The audience now murmured with surprise.

"Then the next thing you know, I'm gone again, just like I was after the roller hit me, and when I wake up I hurt really badly, and I can't move one leg, and I've got this bad pain underneath my body. Well, it turns out I had a—what was it again?"

"Emergency surgery," said Felicia.

"The Upright had to do the . . . whatever it was she just said, because it turns out I was—what was I, Felicia?"

"Bleeding internally," Felicia informed him.

"Now when that happens," Tazar continued with the assurance of an expert, "it's very serious, and in fact you could die if it's not dealt with quickly, and the only way you can stop it is to be cut with a Silver Claw, not to kill you, but to make you better. Also my leg was all banged up and they had to make it stiff so that I wouldn't move it. So I couldn't walk properly, and of course that makes hunting difficult, and anyway I'm in an Upright den, and the only prey was a few scrawny-looking cats that I couldn't get at. So they fed me this stuff out of a cylinder. They just open up the cylinder and out it pops, and it's delicious. Best food I ever had."

Waggit had to smile, because he knew exactly what Tazar was talking about. He had eaten the same kind of food when he had lived with the woman who had saved him from the Great Unknown, and he remembered it being very tasty.

"Anyway," Tazar went on, "this Upright does this for the Petulants of other Uprights who don't have much—what's that stuff called again, Felicia?"

"Money," answered Felicia.

"Yeah, that stuff. And he assumed that Felicia was a Skurdie, so he let her sleep near me. She stayed there for what seemed like many risings, and gradually the pain went away, and the leg got easier to walk on, though it's not back to the way it used to be yet."

"But how did you both escape?" asked Cal.

"We didn't. They just let us go when they thought I was ready," replied Tazar.

"They let you go?" exclaimed Raz with amazement. "You mean this Upright never called the Ruzelas to have you taken to the Great Unknown?"

"No, he just stroked me under the chin, said something to Felicia in his Upright language, and then opened the door and let us out."

"What did he say?" the astonished Raz asked Felicia.

"He said that Tazar was a remarkable dog and that I was very lucky to have him," she replied.

"Yeah," said Tazar. "He was a very decent Upright. His name was Alan."

Of the many gasp-inducing things that Tazar had told the team, nothing beat this last statement. In all the years the dogs had been together, the words "decent" and "Upright" had never left Tazar's mouth in the same sentence.

"But—but—but—you always said there was no such thing as a good Upright," said Little One.

"No," said Tazar, in the tone of voice that a teacher uses with a particularly slow student. "What I said was *most* Uprights are bad. I never said they all are. Look at Felicia here. Nobody could call her a bad Upright, now could they?"

Although none of the team members would have disputed that statement under any circumstances, the complete reversal of Tazar's long-held beliefs about humans so stunned the dogs that none of them could speak anyway.

Waggit, who had been listening to all this in amused silence, now turned to Felicia.

"Thank you, Felicia, for saving Tazar's life and bringing him back to us," he said.

"I didn't do much, really," said Felicia. "We were lucky I found this veterinarian, and even more lucky that he doesn't charge a lot of money, as Tazar said. I'm afraid I'm a bit short at the moment."

This last statement confused the dogs, because Felicia was the tallest person they had ever seen.

"You're not short; you're huge," cried Little Two.

"Well, thank you, Little Two." Felicia chuckled. "I'll assume you meant that in the best possible way. What I meant was I don't have a lot of money at the moment. My family is trying to rein me in and has been a bit tightfisted lately."

Because of Felicia the Tazarians knew of the existence of money, but they had only a vague grasp of what it was and how you used it, and they didn't find it very interesting anyway. What did interest them was the way that Tazar walked as he crossed the meadow to take his first look at the cave. Although he moved almost normally, he had a noticeable limp on his left hind leg. He turned and saw them looking at it.

"Don't worry," he said, "it's a little bit stiff, but it works okay. Felicia says it makes me look rheumatic."

Felicia snorted with laughter. "I didn't say rheumatic; I said romantic. It gives you the air of a bandit."

Waggit could see that the experience the two of them had had during his recovery had brought Tazar and Felicia much closer together, and he had to confess to himself that he felt a twinge of jealousy. Felicia had always been his friend first and foremost, and now there was an intimacy between her and Tazar that he didn't share. He loved the fact that Tazar had changed his attitude to some humans at least, and Felicia especially, but he disliked the feeling of being excluded. He didn't have time to dwell on this, though, because Tazar called him over to the opening of the cave.

"This is fine, Waggit," he said with admiration. "This is really fine. This is the best place we've ever lived. You did well."

"It's very comfortable," Waggit agreed. "There's plenty of space, and it never gets too hot or too cold, and there's water close by."

"What I don't understand," Tazar continued, "is

why there were no dogs living here already. It's so ideal, and there must've been teams that have come through this way, or even a loner or two."

Waggit thought that this wasn't the time to tell him about the Curse.

"We were just lucky, I guess" was all he would say.

The other dogs took Tazar around and showed him where everything was and talked excitedly about the hunting and how you hardly ever saw a human but you could scavenge if you wanted to, and all the other parts of their new life they wanted him to know.

"It's just like the old times," said Raz.

"You're too young to know about old times," said Lowdown.

"Well," Raz corrected himself, "it's just like the Deepwoods used to be when I was first abandoned. You decide what you want for supper and then go get it."

"What do you want for supper?" Cal asked Tazar.

"Hopper," he replied. "I'd love some hopper. That canned food is good, but I missed fresh meat."

"Hopper it is, then," promised Cal.

As a hastily formed hunting party left for the woods to fulfill Cal's promise, Tazar wandered around the cave, sniffing corners and scratching the floor with one paw. The more he inspected their new home, the more he seemed content with what he saw and smelled. He turned to Waggit, who was watching him from the cave's entrance.

"You did well, Waggit," he said. "And I don't just mean by finding this place. What I mean is much more important. If it weren't for you, I wouldn't have moved, not yet, anyway, and probably not until it was too late. You also kept the team together, both before the roller hit me and after. I look around and see how happy and secure they all look, and there's only one reason for that—a good leader."

"Tha-tha-thank you, Tazar," Waggit stammered with embarrassment. "It means a lot to me to hear you say that, though it's not easy being a leader, is it?"

"No, it's not," Tazar agreed, "but every team has to have one."

"Well, I'm glad it's still you," said Waggit.

"So am I, Waggit." Tazar chuckled. "So am I."

Although Waggit felt that Felicia and Tazar had become closer in the time they'd been together, he also realized that he too was closer to his leader because of the time they'd been apart. He now felt like Tazar's deputy and was confident that if and when the team needed a new leader, he would be able to rise to the test. He just hoped that it didn't happen too soon. Waggit followed Tazar out into the bright sunshine of the meadow. From behind him he could see that the dog's injured leg was nowhere near back to normal. As Tazar lay down in the sun's warmth he reminded Waggit a little of Lowdown, although this may have been because Tazar lay down right next to him.

Waggit watched the two old friends chatting to each other, and he felt a little embarrassed about being jealous of the attachment between Tazar and Felicia, or anyone else. Their relationship didn't threaten his own, and he felt happy about the affection that had formed between them, two creatures he was very fond of. The rest of the afternoon passed peacefully until the return of Cal, Raz, Little One, Little Two, Gordo, and Magica, all proudly bearing supper—and it was rabbit.

That evening's meal was a joyous affair. The team was back together again; their new home was splendid; their leader had recovered; they were in the company of their favorite person; their stomachs were full and likely to remain that way for some time. This wasn't just like the old times that Raz had spoken about—this was *way* better. As Waggit sat there enjoying the food and camaraderie he felt a true contentment. He had even forgotten about the Curse of Damnation Hill.

Unfortunately, the Curse of Damnation Hill had not forgotten about him.

18

A Turn for the Worse

Things started to go wrong shortly after Felicia and Tazar returned. At first they were minor incidents, the kinds of things that often happen in everyday life. Raz pulled a muscle while hunting and had to limp home on three legs. Then a branch snapped off a tree and hit one of the dogs. Fortunately it hit Gordo, whose heavy padding helped protect him, and actually did more damage to the branch than it did to him. Cal had a narrow escape while scavenging near one of the ball fields. A police car had cruised by just as he had his head and the top half of his body stuck in a garbage can. He managed to extricate himself and slip past the cops just in the nick of time. And though there was nothing unusual about any of these events, their frequency became alarming.

But then things started to get much more serious. Alona suddenly became very sick, and nobody knew why. She couldn't eat, was feverish, and got alarmingly weak in a very short span of time. She had deteriorated to the point where she could no longer stand when Felicia decided to take her to Alan, the veterinarian who had treated Tazar. She was too frail to even sit on the skateboard that had become the team's makeshift ambulance. Felicia had to carry her, which wasn't a problem because Alona had lost so much weight.

For two days the worried dogs heard nothing, and then Felicia returned, by herself. The dogs gathered around, anxious to hear her news.

"It's not good, I'm afraid," she said. "Alan has done a number of tests on her and can't figure out why she's so sick. At the moment he's giving her food and liquids intravenously."

The dogs looked at her blankly.

"I'm sorry, Felicia," said Tazar, "but I don't think any of us understood what you just said."

"Forgive me," replied Felicia. "I'm so worried about her that I forgot you haven't had any experience of this kind of thing before. The bottom line is that Alan doesn't know why she's sick, and the only way he can keep her alive is by putting food into her through a tube that goes straight into her body, instead of through her mouth."

Gordo was now very attentive, always being interested in alternative ways of eating.

"What do we do now?" asked Tazar.

"There's really nothing we can do except wait," replied Felicia. "I told Alan I'd go back in a couple of days to see how she's progressing."

"It's the Curse," wailed Alicia suddenly. "I knew we shouldn't have come here. At least the old park wasn't jinxed like this one is."

"What Curse?" Tazar tersely demanded.

"The Curse the Terminor told Gordo about. Did you know this place is called Damnation Hill? It ain't safe here, I'm telling you."

Tazar turned to Waggit.

"Did you know about this Curse?" he asked.

"Yes," replied Waggit. "One of the Terminors told us about it."

"Why didn't you tell me?" Tazar demanded.

"Well," said Waggit, "it never really came up."

This was true, inasmuch as nobody had spoken about the Curse since Tazar's return. Waggit had thought about telling him many times but was afraid that the leader would be scornful of him taking such nonsense seriously. But now it seemed that taking it seriously had been the smart thing to do.

"Waggit," said Tazar, firmly but without anger, "I have to know everything that happens. Knowledge is the power that allows me to make good decisions. I cannot afford to be blindsided by ignorance. You need to tell me every single thing, no matter how trivial it might seem."

So, feeling somewhat chastened, Waggit told Tazar about the meeting with Cabrol. He also told him that he had ordered the dogs who had been present at the encounter not to tell the rest of the team about the Curse. He gave Gordo a piercing stare when he said this, and now it was Gordo's turn to look shame-faced.

"I suppose I assumed you would think it was silly of

us to be scared by Cabrol," he continued. "I suppose I thought you wouldn't believe in the Curse."

"I've seen too many things in my lifetime that nobody could explain to not keep an open mind," said Tazar. "No, I believe that there are such things as jinxes, and that they can be evil and potent."

Felicia had remained silent during this exchange, but from the expression on her face, it was obvious that she was more skeptical about the Curse than Tazar.

But then, as if to reinforce Tazar's words, the dogs awoke the next morning to find that the spring had stopped running and the water in the pool tasted and smelled bad. It was Gordo who discovered it. He drank more than any other dog on the team, and this was one of the rare days when he was up first. He came back into the cave spluttering and sticking his tongue out, trying to get rid of the taste.

"Ugh, the pool tastes awful today," he complained, "and it seems to be lower than it was."

"If it tastes bad to you," observed Alicia, "then it must really taste bad, 'cause you'd drink anything."

It was true that Gordo would slurp from puddles that other dogs wouldn't go near, so this was a clear indication that the water situation was serious. The rest of the team gathered around the pool. It definitely contained less water than normal, and the reason was obvious. The steady cascade of water that had flowed from the rocks into it no longer did, and the stream that once splashed out the other side and down the hill had dried up. A reliable source of fresh water was vital for the dogs, who could go much longer without food than without drink. However difficult life in their former home had become, one thing they never had to worry about was water.

"Oh dear, Tazar," said Magica. "What are we going to do?"

"We'll find a way out of this," Tazar assured her. "Don't you worry."

"There's always the Wide Flowing Water," suggested Little One.

"The park goes right down to it," added Little Two.

"If you think my old legs are gonna get me down there and back up again every time I need a drink, then you're nuts," said Lowdown. "Even your young limbs are gonna get pretty tired running up and down four or five times a day, not to mention the fact that you're in Upright land down there."

"Not only that," said Waggit, "but the Ductors told us that if we drank it, we would go mad."

All of this was true, but none of them could think of any alternative, which caused Gruff to sigh mournfully.

"This is what comes of listening to uppity young dogs that think they're leaders and their big ideas about change. Stick with what you know, I always say." He moaned.

"We should ask Felicia what she thinks," said Waggit, ignoring this last remark, which was obviously aimed at him.

It was generally agreed that this would be a good idea, and they ran over to the corner of the meadow where she had camped. There is nothing that will get you out of bed quicker in the morning than a pack of dogs barking outside your tent, and it certainly had the required effect on Felicia that morning. She unzipped the door, stumbled sleepily through it, and stretched herself fully awake. The sight of Felicia stretching was always an awesome sight for the dogs, for while they always stretched horizontally, she did it vertically and looked taller than ever.

"Well, dogs, where's the fire?" she asked.

"There's no fire."

"What fire?"

"Did you smell fire?"

The Tazarians were confused.

"I'm sorry," said Felicia, realizing her mistake. "That's an Upright phrase meaning 'what's the panic?'"

"Why doesn't she say what she means?" Gruff asked. "Why does she have to get us all worried about fires that don't exist?"

"Why don't you be quiet," said Alicia sharply, "and let us tell her what the problem is?"

So the dogs did just that. Felicia listened carefully to what they said, and then there was silence. They knew that this meant she was thinking about the situation, mulling over possible solutions, and the dogs knew better than to interrupt her.

After a few moments she said, "This may be more serious than you realize. Even those of you who are capable of running up and down the hill every time you're thirsty, and are willing to risk the Uprights around the ball fields, may find yourselves disappointed. If I'm not mistaken, both of those rivers are saltwater around here, so you couldn't drink from them anyway."

The dogs pondered this information.

"We mustn't forget," said Magica, "that Pilodus said the Wide Flowing Water would suck a dog in and you'd never be seen again."

"This place is cursed all right," mumbled Gruff, only this time nobody disputed him.

"Springs like the one next to the cave often dry up suddenly, and just as often start running again. You can't assume it's because of the forces of evil," Felicia assured them. "You know, we haven't had any rain in a long time."

Apart from the downpour on the first day of their journey, there had been something approaching a drought for several weeks, but the dogs were inclined to believe the "forces of evil" over the force of nature explanation.

"The short-term solution is easy," Felicia continued more cheerfully. "I will go to the store and purchase a large container that I can fill from the water fountains near the ball fields. If I do it once a day, that should be enough to keep you going, and if it isn't, I'll fill it twice a day."

"That's very good of you," said Tazar, "but you're

right. It doesn't solve the problem. We can't be dependent on you for something as vital as water. For one thing, there's still Alona. She needs you to be there for her, and who knows if you might have to stay with her like you did with me?"

"And don't forget, Tazar," Felicia reminded him, "the nights are going to start getting colder pretty soon, and I'm going to have to go south when they do."

"Besides which," Tazar continued, "if we have to rely on an Upright to survive, even one like you, then we might as well all become Petulants and be done with it."

"I honestly don't know what the long-term solution is," said Felicia, "but I'm convinced that there is one, and it doesn't involve moving once again. I mean, apart from anything else, where would you go?"

It was a question that most of the team was thinking and none of them could answer.

While the answer didn't reveal itself in the next couple of days, they were relieved that no other disasters happened. Even though none of the other team members paid any attention to it, Gruff's comment about "uppity young dogs that think they're leaders"

worried Waggit. Although Beidel had initially suggested moving, Waggit had been the first one to
embrace the idea and push for it. Maybe they should
have tried harder to find another solution in the old
park; maybe he had just been trying to increase his
influence with Tazar. Waggit *did* feel responsible for
the team's new home, and on good days this was a
source of pride for him, but on bad days it made him
feel guilty that they had listened to him. He needed
to find a solution to their present situation. But if
there really was a Curse, what could they do about it
but move?

He was in this frame of mind when he went for a
walk by himself in the woods above the cliff. There
were occasions when he needed to talk to Lowdown
about a problem and others when he needed to think
things through by himself, and this was one of the lat-
ter. Also, he liked being alone from time to time. He
realized that since they had been living on the hill, he
had always been too busy to explore its upper reaches.
He was a naturally curious dog, and exploring was fun
for him, so he decided to follow a path he had never
taken before. It hadn't been made by humans and was
probably the work of deer, for their scent was strong

on the trail. It ran over lightly wooded land through which the sun filtered, keeping it warm and friendly. To his left he saw an area of much denser forest. It was dark and mysterious, and the deer path veered away from it as if the creatures who had made it wanted nothing to do with the unlit place. But something drew Waggit toward it, some impulse that came from deep within him.

19

Wisdom from the Ancient One

Waggit took a deep breath and headed toward the dark forest. As he entered it, he could feel the temperature drop and the air get damp. He smelled the powerful aroma of rotting leaves. There was something about this place that was beyond time, where the past, present, and future had no meaning at all. There were no paths here, no evidence that anyone had ever been this way. Because the canopy of leaves was so dense and prevented any light from filtering through them, there was almost no undergrowth.

Also, the trees were spaced farther apart than on the rest of the hill, which made walking much easier than he had anticipated. He had no idea why he was heading in the direction he took, or where he was going, but he followed his instincts.

The forest had the curious effect of being bigger on the inside than it looked from the outside, and Waggit had been walking for what seemed like ages when he saw it. There was a flash of orange at the outer edges of his vision, but when he whirled around, it disappeared. At first he was sure his mind was playing tricks on him, but then he saw it again. In the darkness two orange eyes were watching him. Cautiously he moved toward them, but he never seemed to get any closer, although it appeared they weren't moving. He broke into a run, and suddenly he was in a clearing, one that was covered by the unrelenting ceiling of leaves, making it almost as black as any other part of the forest. His eyes had now adjusted to the lack of light, and on the far side of the clearing he could see the Gray One standing on a fallen tree trunk. Even in the gloom he looked powerful and mysterious, those piercing eyes surrounded by a mane of fur, his strong muscles tight inside his coat. Waggit approached him carefully, aware that he was no match for this being.

"You did well to find me, Waggit" came the voice out of the darkness. "You are a dog of great character."

"I wasn't looking for you," said Waggit. "I didn't know this place existed until now."

"But you are a seeker, and seekers often find what they do not know but which they long for."

"And what do I long for?" asked Waggit.

"You yearn for the Tazarians to be at peace, to have security and stability, but you don't know how to solve the problems that plague them now, so you come here."

"How can you find peace when you live in a place that is cursed and you have nowhere else to go?" he asked the Gray One.

"It will be cursed only as long as you are the Curse's keeper," the Gray One replied.

"What do you mean?" Waggit was puzzled by what the creature said. "The hill was cursed long before we got here."

"And long before you got here, other dogs kept the Curse and gave it its power. It will only exist for as long as you or those who come after you believe in it."

"But so many bad things have happened," protested

Waggit. "Are you telling me that none of them had anything to do with the Curse?"

"Life is full of bad things," replied the Gray One. "You are fortunate that they are outnumbered by the good. Many dogs live with misfortune and only misfortune their entire lives. What has happened to your team is of little importance. Raz pulled a muscle while hunting—well, we've all done that; Alona got sick, but she will recover; and the spring ran dry, not because of any evil intent by an Upright long dead, but because it hasn't rained for many risings. It will rain again, and there are other springs on Gray King Hill."

Waggit was stunned that the Gray One knew all that had happened to the team in the last few days, but what surprised him most was the name that he gave to the area.

"Don't you mean Damnation Hill?" he asked.

"That is what some call it," said the wolf, "but long before it got that name, before Uprights roamed the land, and when creatures long gone lived here, it was named after the Gray King, a being of immense power and wisdom who ruled its woods. You must call it by whichever name you think suits it best."

Waggit fell silent, pondering all that the wolf had

said. It was confusing to be told one thing and then something completely different. The facts were the same, but their meanings were miles apart.

"So what you're saying," he asked after a few minutes of contemplation, "is that if we don't believe in the Curse, no more bad things will happen to us?"

"Bad things will always happen," replied the wolf. "It's the way of the world. But if you believe they are caused by evil, then you are powerless to do anything about them. If you have the courage to face them, they will be vanquished. Follow your destiny, Waggit. Don't let the fears of foolish dogs deflect you from its path."

Then, as had happened the first time that he met the Gray One in the cave, Waggit suddenly felt immensely tired. He lay down on the soft, leaf-strewn forest floor and was asleep in an instant.

He must have slept for several hours, because when he woke up, a reddish gold light was shining at the low angle that indicated it was near day's end. The trees glowed like golden scepters, and the forest was not as cold and mysterious as it had been earlier. He decided that it must be because the sun was flooding under the leaf ceiling at this time of day. There was no sign of the Gray One, so he got up, shook himself, and made his way out of the forest. When he was on the deer path, he turned to look back at where he had been and once again was struck by how much smaller it seemed from the outside than the inside. Then his eye caught something glittering on the far edge of the forest. He could see a fork in the deer path leading toward it, so he cautiously headed in that direction.

It was farther away than it first appeared, but finally he could see it—a rock pool that bubbled up from an underground spring and spilled down the side of the hill. The pool's surface shimmered in the late-afternoon sunlight, and he watched fascinated as the water cascaded through the woods like liquid gold. He realized that its course must take it quite close to the cave, although he couldn't understand why they hadn't found it before. They had roamed all the neighboring areas in search of another water supply when the spring ran dry. Feeling suddenly thirsty, he drank from the pool. The water was sweet and icy cold, and Waggit thought it was the most delicious thing he had ever tasted. Excited about his discovery, he ran back down the path to the meadow, where he found Felicia filling plastic bowls with water for the dogs to drink out of. She looked up as he approached.

"Why, Waggit," she cried. "Where have you been? We almost sent out search parties to look for you."

"I've found another spring, one that's running now," he yelped eagerly, "with a stream that runs down the hill not too far from here."

"That's great news," said Felicia, who was getting a bit tired of hauling water up the hill. "Where is it?"

"As best as I can work out," replied Waggit, "it's over in that direction."

He pointed with his nose to where he thought the stream was located.

"That doesn't make sense," said Tazar. "We've scoured every blade of grass and fallen leaf in that area looking for water. We couldn't have possibly missed it."

When Tazar said "we," he meant the Tazarians rather than himself. Although his broken leg had healed quite well, he still walked with a limp and found it difficult to move quickly through wooded areas. Hunting, which he'd never been any good at anyway, was now completely out of the question.

"That's what I thought," replied Waggit, "but it's there all right. The spring is way up the hill, but the stream was flowing in this direction."

"Let's go look for it now," said Raz, all fired up and ready for adventure.

"Yeah, let's," agreed Cal.

"No, it's nearly dark," warned Tazar. "The last thing we want is anyone getting injured crashing through the woods."

Everyone thought that waiting was the sensible thing to do, even Cal and Raz, after some initial groans of disappointment.

"First thing in the morning," said Little One, "as soon as we get up . . ."

". . . we'll go look for it," said Little Two.

And that was exactly what they did.

At first light they left Felicia, Tazar, Lowdown, and Gruff at the meadow. Even Alicia wanted to help search out the stream, mostly because she hated the way the water tasted in the plastic containers. They broke into three groups, each taking one section of the hill on the western side of the caves. Of course, the dogs didn't know east from west; they just knew the side of the hill where the light went late in the day. The weather continued to be dry and warm, and the dogs agreed to meet back at the meadow when the sun was directly overhead. Waggit, Magica, and Gordo took the highest section, Cal and Raz the middle, and Alicia, Little One, and Little Two the lowest part.

Waggit was confident that he would find the stream straightaway, and he and Magica ran into the woods, noses twitching and ears pricked, leaving Gordo to lumber behind yelling for them to wait. Evidence of the recent lack of rain was everywhere, from the dust the dogs kicked up to the crackly brown ferns beneath their paws. They worked systematically, going backward and forward just as they would if they were trying to pick up the scent of their prey when hunting. Every so often Waggit would stop and lift his nose into the air, trying to detect the smell of water, which is quite strong to a dog. The three animals worked their section for several hours, sniffing and listening for the sounds a stream would make as it ran down the hill, but to no avail.

"We should be getting back to the meadow," said Magica, looking at the sun that was high in the sky. "Maybe the others had better luck."

"I don't understand it," said Waggit, his brow wrinkled in a frown. "It has to be here somewhere. I saw it, and it was definitely coming in this direction."

"Well, the woods can be confusing sometimes,"

Magica assured him. "Perhaps it was farther over than you thought."

Waggit was pretty sure that it wasn't, but there was no point discussing it now, and the three of them returned to the meadow. When they arrived, they saw that the rest of the team had returned before them, and from the looks on their faces, their searches had been no more fruitful.

"No luck?" Waggit asked Cal and Raz.

"Nothing," Cal replied.

"You neither?" He turned to Little One and Little Two.

"Nothing," they replied in chorus.

"And don't think we didn't try," screeched Alicia. "I ain't ever walked as far as we did today, and I ain't gonna do it again."

And with that said, she lay down with her back to them all.

"Waggit, are you sure the stream was running down that side of the hill?" asked Tazar. "It's easy to get disoriented in the woods. Maybe it was coming down the other side."

"It can't have been," Waggit reassured him, "because I saw it close to the time of darkening and it was still catching the sunlight. No, it must have been that side."

He looked at the faces of the team and realized that doubt was creeping in, doubt that the spring, the rock pool, and the stream existed outside of his imagination.

"I tell you, I saw it," he protested. "I even drank from it."

"Waggit," said Lowdown in a quiet, calm voice, "if you say you saw it, we believe you; it's just that maybe we ain't looking in the right place is all we're saying."

But Waggit knew in his heart of hearts that wasn't all they were saying.

"I'll find it," he said. "I'll find it by myself."

And he turned and left the meadow, retracing the steps he had taken the day before.

20

The Death of the Curse

Waggit walked disconsolately back up the hill. He knew that what he had seen was real. He could even remember the sensation of the icy, clear water in his mouth and how delicious it had tasted. He was sure that if he returned exactly the way he had gone, then he would find the rock pool, and from there he could follow the path of the stream down until it passed through an area that he recognized. Maybe he could howl to attract the attention of the others until they found him. It was worth a try.

The path was steep, and he was feeling tired from the frustrating search of the morning, but he was determined to solve the mystery of the missing stream. The journey seemed much longer and more difficult than the first time he had made it, but he realized that it was he who had changed, not the terrain. He was no longer excited about what he might find, but fearful of what he might not.

The trouble with woods is that they all look alike, and if it hadn't been for the deer path he was following, he would have had no way of knowing whether or not he was in the same place as yesterday. Then he saw where the trees changed from woodland to forest, and the path veered away from the darkness. What he couldn't see was the fork in the path that led to the pool. He kept going, hoping that it would reveal itself, but soon he realized he had gone too far, and he started to backtrack.

He hadn't gone far when suddenly he found it. If you approached it going up the hill, ferns and other low-growing foliage hid it, but as you came back down, it was obvious for all to see. What wasn't obvious was where the pool was. He walked slowly down the fork in the path, keeping his senses alert for any sign of water. The sunny day had clouded over and the light was no longer bright, giving a gloomy feel to his surroundings.

He heard it before he saw it—the chiming sound of the stream as it splashed over rocks. Then he saw the pool, no longer shimmering like burnished gold, but as black as the rock in which it lay. He went to its edge and sniffed. It still smelled clear and sweet, and he lapped at it eagerly. When his thirst was quenched, he moved to the side of the pool where the stream gushed over the edge as it began its journey down the hill. The drop was quite steep, but his determination to discover its course was stronger than any fear he felt as he began to scramble down alongside it.

The going was hard. At times the hill fell away almost in a sheer precipice, so steep that he had to watch carefully where he was going to keep himself from tumbling head over paws. Because he had to keep his head down, he tracked the stream as much by sound as sight, following its gurgling with his ears as his eyes concentrated on the ground beneath him. Suddenly the noise changed to a hollow rushing sound, and he stopped and looked up. Then he saw with horrible clarity why they hadn't been able to find the stream. A few feet in front of him it disappeared down a large opening in the rock and continued on its way underground. By the time it got anywhere near the cave, it was deep below the surface of the earth

He was bitterly disappointed. Why didn't things work out the way he wanted them to? The cave and the meadow were perfect places for the team to live, but without water they were useless. They could move up to the pool, but there was no shelter, no open space, and Lowdown for one would never be able to make the journey. The whole situation was too frustrating. He had to get back to the team to deliver the bad news, but even this was hard. He couldn't return the way he had come because it was too steep, so he had to cut across in the direction of the deer path. The stones beneath his paws were loose, causing him to stumble frequently. Thorns scratched his skin, and roots concealed gaps that could trap his feet and cause him serious injury if he wasn't careful. He finally made it to the path and despondently trudged back to the meadow. The dogs were excited to see him but worried by his dejected appearance.

"You didn't find it, did you?"

"Yes, I did."

"That's great! Does it come down this way?"

"It does."

"Can you show us?"

"No."

"Why not?"

"By the time it gets near here, it's way underground."

"That's why we couldn't find it?"

"That's why."

"Oh no!"

Felicia came over and stroked his head in sympathy.

"Poor Waggit," she consoled him. "You must be so disappointed, and you tried so hard, but you know you did the best you could, and that's all anyone can do. There are some things that are out of our control and always will be."

Although he knew she was saying this with the best intentions, for the first time in his life he found her really annoying. He wandered over to their rock pool, but it was still dry. Tazar saw how upset Waggit was and came up to him.

"She's right, you know," he said. "You did everything you could. Sometimes things just don't work out. Don't worry. We'll solve this somehow."

Just then Alicia, who had been napping in the back of the cave and had missed the entire conversation, came out yawning and stretching.

"So," she yelped, "did ya find it?"

"He did," said Gordo glumly, "but it's underground and you can't get to it."

"Yeah, well, what did ya expect?" she continued, almost pleased at Waggit's failure. "We ain't gonna get any lucky breaks in this place 'cause it's cursed."

Waggit whirled around and looked her straight in the eyes.

"How do you know this place is cursed?" he snarled. "Do you believe everything Gordo tells you because he believes everything some know-it-all Terminor tells him?"

Alicia was taken aback by the anger in Waggit's voice.

"Well, no, but all these things that've gone wrong—the spring drying up and Alona getting sick and everything else. I mean," she defended herself, "it seems like there's a curse."

"There's only a curse if you believe in it," said Waggit.

"I do believe in curses," Gruff chimed in. "I've seen too much trouble happen in my life not to."

"Yeah, well, you've seen trouble where there wasn't none," said Lowdown, who had joined the fray, "and you've enjoyed every minute of it. I'm with Waggit. The only curse is the one you put upon yourself."

"Oh, well, what about that Upright who was killed by the Wild Yellows?" sneered Alicia, having regained some of her composure.

"How do you know there ever was an Upright?" asked Waggit. "We have only the word of one Terminor, who was told by another dog, who was told by yet another dog, and so on and so on. How do you know that Wild Yellows were ever on this hill? Have you ever seen them or any evidence that they were ever here?"

Since the answer to this question was no, Alicia remained sulkily silent. All the other dogs had now gathered around Waggit, interested in what he was saying.

"When I first joined this team," he continued, "Tazar told me that we controlled our own destinies, that the whole point of being a free dog was taking charge of your life and living it as best you could without being pushed around by others, whether they were Uprights or other dogs. If you believe your life is being ruled by a curse, aren't you giving up that freedom? If some stories told to you by a dog you don't even know stop you from believing you can do anything you want, then what's the point of being a free dog? Why not just become a Petulant? It's a lot easier in many ways. Remember, I know."

Waggit looked around. In front of him the entire team was looking up, hanging on his every word. They were literally looking up at him because, without even thinking about it, he was standing on a rock, just as Tazar did when he addressed the team. In fact Tazar was the only dog in the pack who wasn't gathered around. He was standing a little way off next to Felicia, a look of pride on his face. Tazar knew that a great leader had to share power in order to strengthen it, and that the stability of a team depended upon having another dog ready to take over should anything happen to him. After the disappointment of his son's betrayal he had put all his hopes in Waggit, and now he was seeing all his wishes coming true.

Waggit hadn't meant to make a speech, but Alicia's whiny comment had struck a nerve in him. The words of the Gray One were ringing in his head, and they had to come out.

"There are many things in our lives we can't control. We can't control the way Uprights behave, especially the Ruzelas. We can't even stop Felicia going to South every Chill, and we can't make the Long Cold go away. What we can control is our fear and our belief in ourselves, our ability to survive whatever we have to. We've overcome many obstacles in the past, and we'll do so in the future, but only if we truly believe we can. I've been told that long before this hill was called Damnation Hill it went by the name Gray King Hill, and it was named after a very wise creature. So let's celebrate the death of the Curse; let's give our home back its old name, and forget it was ever called by another."

The team broke out into an uproar of yips and howls, which is the closest dogs get to cheering. And as they did there was a loud clap of thunder above them, and it began to rain.

21
Life Is Good

And it rained; and it rained; and it rained. Waggit had never seen so much rain. For more than two days the dogs stayed in the cave, only venturing out to hunt or scavenge, neither of which produced much to eat. Their prey was staying at home until the storm abated, as were the visitors to the ball fields, so food was short. The dogs didn't mind too much, because they knew the rain was needed to break the long drought. It was so torrential at times that Felicia abandoned her tent and moved into the cave. There was plenty of room, and it remained completely dry even during the most intense downpour. If the truth were told, they liked having her lanky figure sprawled out among them. The sound of her soft snoring lulled them to sleep each night, along with the constant sound of the rain.

Its patter became a backdrop of noise that they tuned out after the first few hours, but on the second day of the storm Gordo thought he heard another sound. He was on Eyes and Ears duty that night, guarding the mouth of the cave. Even to his simple brain this seemed unnecessary. It was unlikely that anyone would be out in such conditions, and even if they were, he would have difficulty seeing them through the torrents that fell and the mist they caused. But Tazar was strict about sentry duty and insisted that someone was posted at all times.

The sound Gordo could hear was water, but it was a different noise from that of the rain. He poked his head out of the cave in curiosity and was instantly soaked. He was not a dog bothered by discomfort, however, and he figured that if his head was wet, the rest of his body might as well be and went out into the meadow. It was pitch-black, but he walked in the direction of the sound and then fell with a loud splash into the previously empty rock pool. He sat there for a second before he realized that his head was being pounded by a constant flow of water. He got up and ran back into the cave, showering its occupants as he did, causing barks and growls as the previously dry, sleepy dogs became wet and awake.

"The spring!" he yelled. "The spring!"

"What about the spring?" someone mumbled grumpily.

"It's running again!" cried Gordo. "It's really running again."

All the dogs ran out of the cave to see for themselves—well, actually not all of them. Alicia said she'd take their word for it. There were yelps of joy; their home was once again perfect, and they wouldn't have to even think about moving. Their problems seemed over.

Except for one. The question of Alona's recovery remained unresolved. The weather was so bad that it had prevented Felicia from leaving the hill to go to the animal hospital where their sister was being cared for.

"It's okay," she assured them. "Alan's a good man, and he'll make sure she gets everything she needs. We'll find out soon enough, when the weather lifts."

True to her word, when the rain finally stopped, she made her muddy way down the hill and disappeared into the surrounding city. As so often happens, the day after the storm was completely clear. The sky was that intense blue that comes only when the air is dry; the temperature was mild, and the sun was warm without becoming too uncomfortable. The dogs lay around contentedly grooming or napping, lulled by the comforting sound of water running into and out of the refilled pool. They all took turns drinking from it and declared it to be sweeter and more delicious than ever. Waggit and Lowdown lay next to each other in the meadow. Waggit chewed a stick, while Lowdown scratched under his chin.

"How come you know the hill was called Gray King Hill before it was called Damnation Hill?" Lowdown suddenly asked.

"Somebody told me," Waggit answered.

"A dog somebody?" Lowdown continued.

"Sort of," replied Waggit.

There was silence while Lowdown thought about this.

"Who was this sort of dog who told you?" he asked after a couple of minutes.

"Just somebody I met," Waggit replied.

"Where'd you meet him?" Lowdown was relentless.

"Will you stop?" cried Waggit. "It was just somebody I met."

Another silence followed.

"It was a Gray One, wasn't it?" said Lowdown eventually.

"What makes you say that?"

"'Cause you asked about whether I believed in them and 'cause only Gray Ones can remember far enough back to know what this place was called before," Lowdown said.

"The fact of the matter is," replied Waggit, "I don't know if I met him or not. If I did, it was twice, but each time it seemed like a dream."

"That's how it is with Gray Ones, or so I've been told," said Lowdown. "I've never met one myself, but I'd like to before I die."

"You wouldn't want to meet this one, not where he lives," Waggit assured him. "He's in the forest way up the hill, and even I found it a tough climb. You might want to see one before you die, but you wouldn't want to die doing it."

"No, I suppose you're right." Lowdown sighed. "That's the problem with having old, short legs."

"Well, you never know," said Waggit, trying to console his friend. "In the future you may be fit enough to get there."

"Waggit," said the old dog, "most of my future's behind me. I ain't ever gonna be fitter than I am right now. Still, it would've been nice to see one. Not many dogs do, you know—in fact there's some who'll tell you they don't exist at all."

"Well, I think this one exists," Waggit assured his friend. "It's strange, though—he lives by himself and looks quite old. I suppose he still hunts, but I've never seen him out."

"Maybe they ain't like us," said Lowdown. "Maybe they don't need food."

"It's a possibility," Waggit agreed, and went back to chewing his stick. The good thing about stick chewing was that it cleared the mind and stimulated thought. Waggit considered what Lowdown had said—if he really wanted to see the Gray One but was unable to make the journey up the hill, maybe Waggit could persuade the wolf to come down and visit Lowdown. Although the Gray One didn't look much like a visiting kind of an animal, it might be worth a try. He decided to go back to the forest at the first possible opportunity.

But all plans to do anything were put on hold by the joyful return of Felicia and Alona later that afternoon. Alona was still very weak, and it had taken them a long time to walk from the animal hospital back to the meadow, but she was looking much better than the day she left. Alan, the veterinarian, had told Felicia that he had no idea what the cause of the illness was, but he suspected it was some sort of a virus. The dogs had no idea what a virus was but vowed to be on the lookout for any others and to bite them at first sight. Whatever the reason for her sickness, time and Alan's treatment seemed to have done the trick, and he had declared her well enough to return home. Had he known where she lived, he might have been more reluctant to release her from his care. Alona was happy to be back with her brothers and sisters, and said that their company was the best medicine she could possibly have. The dogs wanted to know about everything that had happened to her in the hospital.

"Well," she said shyly, "when I first got there, I felt so sick that I really didn't know what was happening.

All I knew was that Dr. Alan kept poking me and sticking things in me, and I would have been afraid if it hadn't been for Felicia being there all the while."

"Same thing happened to me," said Tazar, who preferred the spotlight to be on him. "He stuck *huge* things in me. I wasn't afraid, of course," he added, in case the thought had crossed anyone's mind. Felicia thought it better not to mention the terrible yelping noise Tazar had made every time a needle came near him.

"When Felicia left I was a bit scared," Alona continued, "because I'd never been inside an Upright's den before, but all the Uprights who were there were very kind to me. There was one who reminded me of Tazar because she was bossy, and her coat was the same color, but she was very gentle and nice."

"Oh, her," said Tazar. "Yes, she was my favorite."

"I liked Dr. Alan the best," said Alona. "He's so kind and he has very soft, warm paws."

"Yes," agreed Tazar, "he's a good guy. I'd go back to him anytime."

By now the team was getting used to Tazar's conversion to a "people-friendly" dog, but this seemed to be going a bit far even for him. That evening Felicia gave one of her celebratory feasts to mark the reunion of all the dogs in their new home. The first summer she had spent with the team, these banquets had been a frequent feature of life in the park. This year, because of her lack of money, she hadn't been able to afford them. But to celebrate the return of Alona and the flowing of the spring, as well as Raz's leg healing, she decided to splurge on a meal to remember. She went off to the market, and the dogs settled down to await her return. Toward the end of the afternoon they heard her before they saw her—humming tunelessly, as she often did. Then her head popped up above the edge of the meadow, followed by arms laden with plastic bags from which delicious smells wafted.

It was quite dark by the time she had assembled the food. Unlike their former home, this park had no lights illuminating the pathways, and although the city itself gave off a glow, in the meadow it was too black to see very much. Gordo always said you didn't have to see food in order to eat it, but Felicia had decided to buy some candles to help the diners anyway, and to stop Alicia, the other chowhound in the team, from stealing her neighbor's food under the cover of darkness. Most of the dogs had never seen candles, and they were greeted with "oohs" and "aahs" as if they were the latest in modern technology.

The team thought the meal was excellent, being the usual mixture of dog and human food that Felicia put together so deftly. There were wooden skewers of slightly charred meat that she dished out one to a dog, with the skewers removed of course. She had also purchased some chorizo sausages with a wonderful smoky flavor and cans of the dog food that Tazar had liked so much during his stay in the hospital. In addition to all this, there were several different kinds of ham, rawhide chews, and crunchy dog biscuits. You could always tell the success of a meal by the lack of conversation that accompanied it. If Gruff wasn't complaining about how food didn't taste like it used to or Tazar wasn't sermonizing about the superiority of dogs, then you knew that the provisions were pretty good. Tonight the only sounds to be heard were chewing, the smacking of lips, and the occasional, but discreet, belch or hiccup.

Waggit paused in eating his own meal and looked around at Felicia and the dogs in the warm, flickering light of the candles. A mushy feeling of affection came over him, causing a smile to flicker over his lips as he observed their various quirks and characters. That he loved all of them was without question, even Alicia and Gruff. But there was one who would always be his special friend. He watched Lowdown as he tried to get the better of a large piece of rawhide. His old teeth were having difficulty chewing it, and every so often he would shake it ferociously in his jaws as if it wasn't quite dead. At that moment Waggit became even more determined that if his old friend wanted to see a Gray One before he died, he would do everything in his power to make it happen.

22

Brown One Meets Gray One

The morning after the feast Waggit slipped away from the team unnoticed and made his way back up the hill. The path was familiar to him by now, although it wasn't any easier to climb because of this. When he finally saw the forest, he was panting, because the day had become unusually warm again. He resisted the temptation to quench his thirst in the pool he now knew was there and headed straight into the forest. At least it looked like the forest from the outside, as black and foreboding as ever; but when he entered it, there appeared to be a change that was slight but still perceptible. It was neither quite as dark nor as cold as he remembered it. Sunlight shone in dappled patches, and the leaf canopy didn't look as all-encompassing as before.

There was no sign of the Gray One anywhere, nor was there any evidence that such a creature had ever roamed these parts. In fact one thing that Waggit did notice was the presence of many small animals, something he realized had been missing from his previous visit. He tracked back and forth, using his nose to try to detect a smell, his eyes on the lookout for broken branches or flattened foliage, anything that would indicate the existence of a large wolf, but there was nothing. He had no idea how long he kept this up, but it was some time before he finally accepted that the Gray One wasn't there, if he ever had been. Maybe the dogs who said there was no such thing were right and Waggit had imagined him. But he hadn't imagined the Gray One. He had seen him and spoken to him, and yet he still wasn't sure such a creature existed. It was all very confusing.

It was in this perplexed state of mind that he began to make his way back down the hill. He always found going down more difficult than going up, and today was no different. It was almost as if the tree roots and ferns were trying to trip him up; but he wasn't in a hurry, so he took his time getting back home. The deer path dropped sharply as it passed by the meadow's outer edge, causing him to run down the last few feet. What he saw then stopped him dead.

On the far side Felicia and most of the rest of the team were gathered around something or someone lying on the ground. Waggit's heart froze, because he knew exactly what they were looking at—it was Lowdown, and he wasn't moving. Waggit raced over to the worried onlookers. When he got a closer look at Lowdown, his first emotion was one of relief—he clearly wasn't dead. He was just lying there unable to get up, but there was a peaceful feeling about him, not one of distress. Waggit turned to Felicia and Tazar, who were standing next to each other in the group, clearly concerned like the rest.

"What happened?" he panted.

"It was weird," said Tazar. "Lowdown suddenly got up and moved here to the edge of the woods, where he never usually goes. I was watching him, and it was almost like he was talking to somebody, but no one was there. Then suddenly he fell over on his side, and when we got to him, he was fast asleep. He only just woke up."

Waggit gently pushed everyone back to give Lowdown as much air as possible, and then went up to the old dog and looked at him in the face.

"Are you okay?" he asked.

"I'm beyond okay," Lowdown replied. "I'll always be grateful to you for sending the Gray One to me. He is truly awesome."

"You saw the Gray One?" Waggit asked incredulously.

"I sure did," replied Lowdown. "He was in the woods just over there. He told me you sent him."

"He did?" Waggit asked even more incredulously.

"Yeah," said Lowdown. "He said you told him I wanted to see a Gray One before I died."

"I did?" Waggit gasped.

"Waggit," said Lowdown, now completely awake, "are you having difficulty understanding me today? Ain't I using language what makes sense?"

"No —I mean yes—I mean, I'm just surprised

he came so quickly," Waggit replied, trying to cover his confusion the best he could. "What did you talk about?"

"Oh, this and that," said Lowdown. "Birth, death, and the things in between."

"How long was he here?" asked Waggit.

"You know, that was the strange thing," Lowdown replied. "I really couldn't say. It was like time stood still—actually more like it didn't exist at all. Then all of a sudden I felt incredibly tired, and the next thing I know, everyone's staring at me like I died or something. But I ain't, as you can see." Indeed, the old dog seemed rejuvenated by the experience.

"Well, you had me worried," said Waggit. "I was sure you'd gone paws up when I saw you."

"Not yet, my friend," Lowdown said, chuckling. "That was one of the things the Gray One told me. He said that everyone has their appointed rising when all this will end but mine ain't yet. He didn't say anything about you, though, so I would tread carefully, if you want my advice."

"What?" cried Waggit. "What d'you mean?"

"I'm joking," Lowdown assured him. "You're too

horribly healthy to worry about anything like that. C'mon, let's go and make sure the others ain't digging out a little hole in the ground for my final resting place."

And with that he got up, shook himself, scratched behind his ear, and went over to Felicia, Tazar, and the other anxious dogs, all of whom made a big fuss about him. He in turn did nothing to dissuade them from telling him how important he was to the team and how worried they had been.

While this was happening, Waggit walked into the woods to where Lowdown had indicated the Gray One had been. There, in between two maple trees, was an indentation made where a large animal had flattened the ferns. At first he thought it could have been Gordo, but there was the same strange odor hanging in the air——a smell ancient and primitive that he now recognized as the scent of the Gray One.

Everyone felt relieved when it was obvious that Lowdown's "episode" wasn't serious. Waggit noticed that the old dog let everyone think that what had happened was the result of his old age, and didn't mention the Gray One at all. Later in the afternoon the two dogs were lying together in the meadow enjoying the late-afternoon sun. Waggit turned to his friend.

"Lowdown?" he said.

"Yes, Waggit," the old dog replied.

"Do you think the Gray One really exists?"

"Did you see him?" asked Lowdown.

"Yes, twice," Waggit replied.

"Well," said Lowdown, "in that case I would say that for you he exists. For me too, for that matter."

"But I mean, does he really exist—flesh and blood exist, so you can touch him? Which I never did, by the way."

"No, me neither," agreed Lowdown, "but that don't mean he wasn't there. Look at those fluffies up there." He pointed his nose to the sky, where the clouds were just beginning to get the touch of gold that marked the approach of day's end. "You can't touch 'em, but you know they're there."

"So why did you see him when nobody else did— not Tazar, not Felicia, not anyone in the team?"

"I dunno," said Lowdown. "Maybe it was because I wanted to see him and they didn't. Maybe we only ever see what we want to."

"It's all very confusing," said Waggit with a sigh.

"It is that," agreed Lowdown, "and the older you get, the more confusing it becomes. You'd think it would be the other way around, but it ain't and that's all there is to it. There's some things you ain't never going to understand, no matter how sharp you are."

Waggit, who didn't feel at all sharp at that moment, decided he would have to accept what Lowdown said as true. He was feeling restless; when things were unresolved, he always felt restless. He didn't like experiences he couldn't understand; they worried him, and he still couldn't make sense of who or what the Gray One was. He wandered over to Tazar, who was getting up and stretching as if preparing to go somewhere.

"What's up, Waggit?" he asked cheerily in greeting.

"Not much," Waggit replied. "You going somewhere?"

"Oh, I thought I might just head on down to the ball fields and see if there's any lost souls who might need a helping paw."

This was something that Tazar did regularly. Toward the end of the day he would go out to look out for any recently abandoned or lost dogs wandering about helplessly in the park who he might rescue. This was how Waggit himself had first met Tazar.

"Can I come with you?" he asked Tazar.

Tazar looked at him. He noted the worried frown that caused wrinkles in the fur above Waggit's eyes, and he could feel the uneasy tension in his body.

"Tell you what," said Tazar. "Why don't you do it instead of me? I've got a few things to attend to here anyway." He didn't say what the things were and Waggit didn't ask. Although the leader enjoyed his solitary rescue missions, the fact of the matter was he rarely found dogs to help. They were either too timid and ran before he could talk to them or the authorities got them first. Waggit was the last dog he had met on one of these expeditions who he had persuaded to join the team. But Tazar's greatest quality as a leader was his instinctive understanding of what his teammates needed, feared, or hoped for. He realized that something had disturbed Waggit, and that giving him a task would take his mind off it.

"Yeah, okay, I'll do it," said Waggit.

"It's okay to go now, but be careful," Tazar warned. "When it's still as light as this, the Uprights tend to hang around after they've played ball, and if there's Uprights, then there's usually a Ruzela or two."

"Don't worry," Waggit reassured him, "I'll be careful."

He rubbed up against Tazar in a gesture of affection and then headed down the hill to see what was happening at the ball fields.

23

Lost and Found

Taking heed of Tazar's warning, Waggit skirted the edges of the ball fields when he came off the hill. This area was fairly safe when it was dark, but with the light of late summer it could remain crowded until quite late. Sure enough, small groups of humans were gathered around benches or seated on the grass, laughing and drinking sodas. He knew that a friendly gesture from one of them could often turn to anger if ignored, and the best strategy was to avoid any contact with people completely. The presence of so many of them also meant that it was unlikely that any abandoned dog would show himself or herself until the park emptied. Or so he thought.

He had settled down under the cover of some shrubs to keep watch until the last of the humans left when a movement caught his eye. In the middle of a group of people who had just finished a softball game he saw a young dog, no more than a puppy really, running frantically from person to person. Each ballplayer reacted differently to the dog's panicked behavior. Some were welcoming and tried to calm the animal down, while others shooed her away. One man threw a stick for her to chase, but the dog was too frantic to be interested, and the stick thrower gave up trying to get her attention.

Waggit watched all this with his heart in his stomach. One reason for his anxiety was that he knew only too well how quickly the young dog could be in danger. All it would take would be a complaint from one of the group to a passing park worker, and the animal could be snatched up in an instant and on her way to the pound. The other reason the animal's actions distressed Waggit was that they reminded him of his own abandonment. He remembered the way that fear had gripped him as he desperately looked for his "owner," a word that Tazar had forbidden him to use ever since his rescue by the team. He knew that in this state of mind the dog wouldn't listen to the instincts that served his species so well and would act rashly out of despair. The frustrating thing was that Waggit could do nothing about the situation but observe. He couldn't put himself in unnecessary danger in attempting to save the animal, because if he did, there would most likely be two dogs on their way to the pound instead of one.

Finally the group of people got up and headed for the park gates on their way home, but to Waggit's dismay the dog followed them. Then a person at the back of the group waved his hand to shoo her away. When the dog paid no attention, the man picked up a stick that was lying on the ground nearby and raised it above his head as if to strike the animal. This had obviously happened to the dog before, because she scuttled away and stood shaking in the middle of the field. The ballplayers had left the park by now, as had most of the other humans, and Waggit thought his heart would break to see the scared and confused animal standing alone as darkness set in.

Very cautiously Waggit moved forward, running low to the ground from cover to cover, a bench here, a trash can there, anything that would mask his movement. For one thing, he didn't want to be seen by one of the few remaining people, but he also didn't want to spook the dog he was trying to rescue. He was now as close to the animal as he could get without being seen. Now he had to take a risk and come out into the open. As casually as he knew how, he sauntered up to the animal from behind.

"Hey," he said casually.

The young dog shot up into the air, and then turned toward him, eyes wide and body quivering.

"Hi—hi—hi," the dog stammered, looking from side to side to see if there was any way of escaping from this new and scary situation.

"My name's Waggit. What's yours?"

"Um, well, let me see," the other dog spluttered. "I can't remember. It's—oh gosh, it's on the tip of my tongue. It'll come back to me, I'm sure it will."

"No matter," said Waggit, his voice remaining low-key. "Where are you heading?"

"I seem to have become separated from my master," the other said, not noticing the way Waggit flinched when he heard the word. "He's around here some-where, I know it."

Waggit watched the young dog with the compassion that only one who has experienced the same fears can give. He looked up at the encroaching dusk.

"It's kind of darkening," he said. "Are you sure he hasn't left?"

"Oh no," said the female. "He wouldn't leave with-out me. We're very close."

"Well, it's going to be hard for you to see him soon," Waggit observed. "I've got a bunch of friends who live here just up the hill. You'd be welcome to spend the night with us if you'd like."

"Oh, that's nice of you, but I'll be heading home now. He's probably very worried, and I think I can find my way back from here."

Waggit sat down and cocked his head to one side.

"You've never been in this park before, have you?" he asked in a soft voice.

The dog said nothing, and that was Waggit's answer.

"You were surprised when he brought you here, am I right?" asked Waggit.

Again there was no reply.

"And did he throw a ball for you maybe, and when you retrieved it and turned to take it back to him, he was gone?"

This time the young female answered yes in the softest of whispers.

Waggit got up and brushed against the scared dog's shaking body, remembering how comforting it had been on the night of his rescue to feel the solid warmth of Tazar's strong form next to him. He then turned and came face-to-face with her, looking straight into those fearful eyes.

"I know this is hard," he said quietly yet firmly, "but you've been abandoned. I don't know why, and it really doesn't matter. What matters is that you understand that the Upright you call your master will never return."

The young creature let out a long, mournful howl. "No!"

The truth was too awful to contemplate, and yet, deep inside her, she knew that it was just that—the truth.

"He wouldn't do that, would he? He wouldn't leave me all alone."

"You're not alone," Waggit reassured her. "You have

many friends near here. You just haven't met them yet."

"How do you know?" the female asked him. "How do you know what happened?"

"Well," replied Waggit, "walk with me and I'll tell you my tale."

And so the two of them started across the ball field and up the hill, he back to his team and she to her new life.

GLOSSARY

Bad water: Gasoline

Bigwater: The reservoir

Change: Turn of seasons

Chill: The first days of winter

The Cold White: Snow

Crossover: Cross streets

Curlytails: Squirrels

Darkening: Sundown

Deepwater: The lake

Deepwoods End: The north end of the park

Eyes and ears: Sentry duty

Far Distant Territories: New Jersey

Feeder: Restaurant

Flutters: Birds

Goldenside: The west side of the park

Gray One: A wolf who may be mythical

The Great Unknown: The dog pound

Hoppers: Rabbits

Loners: Dogs with no team

The Long Cold: Winter

Longlegs: Horses

Long Light: Summer

Luggers: Carriages pulled by horses

Metal Trees: Lampposts

Nibblers: Mice

Petulants: Pet dogs

Realm: Area of the park that is the domain of a team

Rising: Day

Risingside: The East side of the park

Rollers: Cars

Rollerway: Road going through the park

Ruzelas: Anyone in authority—rangers, police, etc.

Scurries: Rats

Silver claws: Knives

Skurdie: A homeless person in the park

Skyline End: The south end of the park

Stoners: Teenage boys

Updowns: Avenues that run north and south

Uprights: Human beings

Warming: Spring

Wide Flowing Water: The Hudson River

Wild Yellow: Coyote

EXTRAS

WAGGIT
FOREVER

Meet the Ductors

One of the problems for the dogs who live in the park is that the park is all they know. Waggit is the only one who has ever been outside its boundaries. So when circumstances force them to find a new home, they have no idea where to go. If Waggit hadn't met Beidel, the chances are they would never have made it to the safe, wooded hill where they now live.

Beidel is the leader of the Ductors, a tough bunch of street dogs who are scary to look at but who have devoted their lives to helping other dogs in distress. They have set up a series of havens, as they call them, where they can safely house the animals they are assisting until they get to their destination. Usually they only move one or two dogs at a time, and so transporting a whole team is new and much more dangerous. The Ductors don't just help dogs in distress out of the goodness of their hearts. Street dogs depend on scraps thrown in Dumpsters or trash cans, and the last thing they want is to have other dogs feeding off of their precious supply of garbage! By helping the dogs move to new locations, the Ductors keep others out of their territory. Beidel also knows that all dogs like to have a job and a purpose in life, and that they are a happier team if they aren't bored and aimless. I know that my two Samoyeds, who are both therapy dogs, love the work they do!

In the five boroughs of New York City, there are an estimated 1.4 million dogs. That's more than there are people in eleven of the states in this country. Despite this, you rarely see stray animals running loose in the streets. If they're like the Ductors, they sleep during the day and move around at night, and the Tazarians have to adapt to this new way of living. Here are the members of the Ductors who make the journey possible.

BEIDEL

Best Attribute: Great and determined leader capable of making tough decisions.

Worst Attribute: Poor personal hygiene and a snob. He only likes to socialize with other leaders like himself.

Favorite Thing to Do: Planning the routes and new locations for the dogs the Ductors are helping.

Least Favorite Thing to Do: Taking part in any of the operations that involve physically moving the dogs from place to place. He believes in giving orders rather than actually doing anything.

Most Memorable Quote: "If certainty is what you demand, then go back to your park and starve. We have no plans that are based on certainty."

DRAGOMAN

Best Attribute: A good lieutenant. He doesn't want to be the leader but is very good at taking charge on street level. He has great ears as well.

Worst Attribute: Obeys Beidel without question.

Favorite Thing to Do: His job. He loves the excitement of the danger and the knowledge that he's good at what he does.

Least Favorite Thing to Do: Waiting for slow dogs to catch up.

Most Memorable Quote: "You are park dogs; you could no more survive on the streets than we could in the woods."

CICERO

Best Attribute: Alert and aggressive, he's a good dog to bring up the rear of a group. He's always concerned about safety.

Worst Attribute: Sometimes too aggressive and jumpy. He often sees danger where there is none.

Favorite Thing to Do: Like the other Ductors, he loves the streets and the thrill of danger.

Least Favorite Thing to Do: Lead a quiet life. He doesn't ever want to go into a park either.

Most Memorable Quote: "Waggit, is it my mistake, or are you carrying on a conversation with that Upright?"

NAVIGA

Best Attribute: An amazing sense of direction most likely due to the part of her that's German Shepherd.

Worst Attribute: Moody and unsocial, she doesn't like interacting with the dogs she's moving.

Favorite Thing to Do: Be by herself.

Least Favorite Thing to Do: Answer a question.

Most Memorable Quote: "Oh, how disgusting! How can you do that?" (When Waggit explains how the Tazarians hunt and eat rats.)

PILODUS

Best Attribute: Alert, focused and has a great sense of smell. Always focused on the business at hand.

Worst Attribute: Doesn't care much for the dogs he's in charge of moving. To him they're just a problem to be solved, and he is quite capable of leaving one behind if the animal becomes a burden (as he would have done with Lowdown if Waggit hadn't gone to rescue him).

Favorite Thing to Do: To move dogs safely on the street and get them to their destination without incident.

Least Favorite Thing to Do: To have to explain himself.

Most Memorable Quote: "If you catch sight of an Upright, either hide under a sleeping roller, or walk, don't run, past them— and whatever you do, *don't look at them.*"

Be a Ductor and Help Animals in Need!
THINGS KIDS CAN DO

When I'm visiting schools people often ask me what inspired me to write the Waggit series. Obviously the story of rescuing my dog Roo from the park was a big part of it, but there was something else. Most of us say we love animals, but often human beings don't take the best care of the creatures that we share our planet with. Sometimes there is a natural disaster that causes terrible distress to dogs and cats, such as the flooding of New Orleans by Hurricane Katrina. But often we are just thoughtless and careless about the animals that surround us.

We might buy that puppy in the pet store window because it's *really* cute without finding out how and where it was bred. This keeps puppy mills in business and causes misery to the dogs they breed from. We may see a stray dog lost and frightened on the side of a highway but not bother to stop because we're in a hurry. It's things like this that were part of the inspiration for Waggit. I wanted to write a novel that made the readers think about how we should treat the creatures whose lives we affect in so many ways. Tazar is wary of Uprights because he's had such awful experiences with them, and in real life "bad" dogs are often only bad because we made them the way they are.

We can do many things to make sure that we treat animals with the love and respect that they deserve. If you're thinking of getting a dog, consider looking for one through the rescue organizations. There are so many dogs in need of good loving homes, and not all of them are mutts. (Although some of the best ones are!) Every breed has its own breed rescue operation, so if you want a specific type of dog you can get one through them. If your heart is set on a purebred puppy, then go to a reputable breeder. The American Kennel Club can steer you in the right direction. For more information about animal rescue, go to my website—www.waggitstale.com.

Of course cats and dogs are not the only creatures that depend upon our kindness and understanding. The way we live often threatens many of the animals we share the earth with. Some of the organizations that help them are listed below.

http://marinebio.org/Oceans/Conservation/local.asp
http://montanakids.com/plants_and_animals/animal_er/
    Things_Kids_Can_Do.htm
http://www.environment.gov.au/biodiversity/threatened/
    publications/kids.html
http://animals.about.com/od/wildlifeconservation/tp/
    helping_endangered_species.htm

If you're a Waggit fan, you probably think about these things already, but maybe your friends don't. So spread the word that it's cool to be kind to animals! They'll thank you for it!

Q&A: Tell us how you write!

How did you make the career switch from magazine picture editor to children's novelist?

I spent most of my career in photography. I was a photojournalist for many years, traveling the world and photographing some amazing things. One of my favorite assignments was when I went on the Iditarod dog sled race in Alaska for *Newsweek* magazine. Two weeks with gorgeous dogs was my idea of heaven, even if it was thirty degrees below zero! When I stopped being a photographer I became a picture editor (that's the person who chooses which pictures to put in a magazine). I did this for many years, and then I started writing about photography, in magazines and online, finally producing two books on the subject—*Shooting Under Fire* and *Paparazzi*.

I've always written, ever since I was a kid and first wrote an outline of the story of *Waggit* when I was working as a photographer in 1983. It wasn't until I found what I'd written over twenty years later that it finally got published. That was when I discovered that writing for children was the thing that I love to do the best. I have much more fun writing for children than adults. I don't know why—maybe children are just more fun than adults!

What is your writing routine?

I live on a farm in Connecticut, and like all farms, mine has lots of little buildings around the farmhouse. I write in one of them. It's a beautiful place to work, with views over the fields to the wooded hills behind them. I go there after breakfast and write until lunchtime. Sometimes the dogs go with me, but if it's a sunny day they usually prefer to play outside. I try to write

8

a thousand words a day. Sometimes I hit my target, and on rare occasions I'll write even more than that. There are other times when I can barely manage four or five hundred words. If the words are flowing I'll continue writing in the afternoon, but often I take a break and answer email from the website or pay bills (yuck!) and all the other things you have to do when you are a grown up!

What is your favorite thing to eat or drink while writing?
Coffee is a *must* first thing, but I limit myself to two cups. I was born and brought up in England, so tea is still an important part of my daily routine, especially around four in the afternoon. I think it's a genetic thing! Eating is a real problem. I don't know why, but writing makes you *really* hungry, and the need to snack is sometimes overwhelming. I find that nuts are good to satisfy the urge, but so are chocolate chip cookies!

What do you do when you need a writing break?
I'm trying to teach myself Italian with a program on my computer, and so I will take half an hour to do the next lesson. It's a great way to clear my mind. I also love music, but I find it too distracting to play when I'm writing, so sometimes when I take a break I'll listen to something on my iPod.

What do you do if you get writer's block?
Writer's block is real. There's nothing worse than looking at a blank screen on the computer when your mind's equally empty. It sometimes seems as if your brain has seized up. The best thing for me to do when this happens is to take the dogs for a walk around the fields, or, if it's in the summer, to go for a swim. I also love to ride my beautiful horse. He's a redhead

called Will (short for Will Work For Food!) and he lives in a barn just down the road from me. Some form of exercise always seems to free up my mind again, and then I can get back to work.

The character of Waggit was based on your real-life dog Roo. How did you come up with the other characters that weren't based on real animals?

One of the questions I'm constantly asked when I do a school visit is "How did you come up with of the names of the dogs, or the adventures they have?" It's the hardest question to answer because it involves imagination, and nobody has ever been able to explain to me exactly what imagination is. Some of the characters are based upon people I know rather than dogs I know. Unfortunately I've met a lot of Alicias and Gruffs in my lifetime, but I've also been blessed to know some Waggits, Tazars, and Lowdowns as well. As for the names, many of them just pop into my head, and often the book ends in a completely different way from how I thought it would. It's that pesky imagination thing at work again.

Want more by Peter Howe?

Here's a sneak peek at his next book,

WARRIORS OF THE BLACK SHROUD

Walker felt himself tumbling through blackness. He knew Eddie was ahead of him, but he couldn't tell where. The darkness was deeper and more frightening than any he had ever experienced. He didn't know where he was going or what was happening. Sometimes he felt a floor beneath his feet, and then it vanished and he was floating like a lost space explorer. What if he drifted like this forever? He tried not to panic, but it was hard.

Suddenly his feet hit solid ground with a thud. He swayed, trying to regain his balance, and looked around to get his bearings. Then he rubbed his eyes and stared again to make sure that what he saw wasn't some weird dream. He had landed in an ancient-looking city completely surrounded by high walls. Simple, low-roofed houses lined the wide avenue where he was standing. Only one building was bigger than the rest. It looked like a castle, and from its highest turret flew a flag that bore a sunlike symbol.

The sky above his head was the same inky blackness through which he had just fallen, but down here everything dazzled with light. In front of him a group of people watched a juggler keep a stream of balls flying from his hands in an arc above his head. Each ball glowed like a tiny planet, and so did the juggler and his audience. Everything was alive with light—the people, the buildings, even the flowers that edged the lawns in front of every house sparkled in their beds.

In the dark sky dozens of silver birds wheeled and soared, their broad wings catching the same wind currents that moved the flag. Their feathers were mirrored, and they glittered against the blackness. A young boy was walking down the street leading a baby dragon on a leash. It hopped along beside him, and every so often it would let out a huge plume, not of fire but a cloud of bright light. Then Walker heard the sound of hooves and turned to see a pure white horse with a long, wavy mane and a tail that almost touched the ground. Mounted on its back was a man dressed in armor that was mirrored like the birds' wings. In one hand he held a long, shiny lance, on top of which fluttered a pennant with the same emblem as the flag. The man bowed to Walker.

"Greetings, my lord," he said. "You are most welcome to Nebula."

This wasn't the usual way grown-ups spoke to Walker, but it didn't matter because he wasn't really listening. His whole concentration was focused on a spot midway between the horse's eyes. Protruding out of the center of the animal's forehead was a single short horn.

"Yes," said a familiar voice behind him, "it is what you think it is. They always get it wrong in books. They make the horn much too long. The poor creature's head would tip forward if it were any bigger. But then, they often get things wrong in books, I've found."

Walker whirled around to see Eddie leaning on his long, fearsome sword. Eddie also shone with a brilliant light, and the *B* on the Boston Red Sox jacket he always wore gleamed like a neon sign.

"Eddie," Walker cried, "everything is glowing, even you!"

"Of course!" said Eddie. "We all do here. Without light we would suffer a fate worse than a thousand deaths. You're glowing yourself, as a matter of fact."

Walker glanced down and, sure enough, all his clothing and every part of his skin radiated a soft light. He lifted one hand in front of his eyes, turning it as if it weren't part of his body at all. It was strange, but also kind of wonderful.

"That's the way things are in Nebula," Eddie went on. "There are no days here and no nights, either. This is how it is all the time. We live in light but we don't forget that the dark is always present just past the other side of the city walls, and it could take over at any moment. That's why you're here. You have an appointment to see the king. We must hurry. He's waited long enough to meet you."

Photo by Anthea Disney

PETER HOWE is the author of WAGGIT'S TALE and WAGGIT AGAIN. He was born in London, lived in New York for thirty years, and currently resides with his wife and two dogs. He is a former *New York Times Magazine* and *Life* magazine picture editor, and he is the author of two books on photography: SHOOTING UNDER FIRE and PAPARAZZI. His first book for children, WAGGIT'S TALE, is based on the real life of his dog Roo, whom he found abandoned in Central Park in 1981.

For exclusive information on your favorite authors and artists, visit www.authortracker.com.